A DREAM COME TRUE

Jess inherits an idyllic cottage in Cornwall and is determined to begin a new life. But there are surprises waiting. Someone is entering the cottage each time she goes out. Are they hoping to drive her away? If so, why? Can she risk abandoning everything she knows to move away from her parents? Dan, her new neighbour, and his family are persuasive — and she could see a future for herself in Cornwall . . . if she can get over the problems.

CHRISSIE LOVEDAY

A DREAM COME TRUE

Complete and Unabridged

LINFORD
Leicester

First published in Great Britain in 2008

First Linford Edition
published 2009

British Library CIP Data

Loveday, Chrissie.
   A dream come true
   - - (Linford romance library)
   1. Cornwall (England: County)- -Fiction.
   2. Love stories. 3. Large type books.
   I. Title II. Series
   823.9′2–dc22

   ISBN 978–1–84782–869–9

Published by
F. A. Thorpe (Publishing)
Anstey, Leicestershire

Set by Words & Graphics Ltd.
Anstey, Leicestershire
Printed and bound in Great Britain by
T. J. International Ltd., Padstow, Cornwall

A Surprise For Jess

'I just don't understand why *Blakes and Jenkins, Solicitors*, are writing to me, Mum.'

'Oh, for goodness' sake, Jess, open the thing and put me out of my misery. I've been waiting all day to find out what's in that letter.'

Jess turned the heavy envelope over and tore it open. 'Apparently there's a Will and I've been left something. The letter says the enclosed will make it clear.'

'Let me look,' Jess's mum, Sarah said. She skipped through the letter. 'Typical lawyer jargon. But, yes, it looks as if Aunt May has left you something. I wonder what? She was very fond of you.'

'She was a sweet soul. I got quite

close to her that year I went down to stay with her.'

Jess remembered the summer holiday when she had gone to Cornwall to look after the lady she called Auntie May. She was actually a distant cousin of her father's, but she had always called her Auntie.

She remembered the mixed feelings she'd had at the time. She had been about to begin her second year at university in October and needed a holiday job.

★　★　★

'How about an all-expenses paid trip to Cornwall? You'd get food and lodging and a bit of pocket money and you'll have some time to yourself to enjoy Cornwall,' her father had said one evening, waving a letter at Jess.

'What's the catch?' Jess had said suspiciously.

'Remember Auntie May? We used to go to her for our holidays in Cornwall when you were little. Well, she's had an accident and needs someone to look after her for a few weeks. She's got hordes of dogs that all need walking and she can't bear the thought of putting them in kennels. Besides, it would cost a fortune. So . . . what do you think?'

'How long would she need me? And the phrase, pocket money, doesn't sound like it would help much towards my savings. I really don't want to take on any more student loans.'

'She says you wouldn't have to spend anything,' her father told Jess. 'But I'm thinking more of poor old Auntie May struggling on. Anyway, you love dogs and would be doing her such a favour.'

Jess had, of course, gone down to Cornwall, and remembered spending a lovely few weeks in Auntie May's delightful cottage. Her aunt had broken her ankle and was hobbling about on crutches. Her assorted collection of mostly rescue dogs had taken up a lot of Jess's time, what with walking, feeding and brushing them. Auntie May didn't need much help, except with the cooking and some basic household tasks. But she was undemanding and insisted that Jess should spend part of most days either on the beach or doing something for herself.

Jess had borrowed her aunt's little car to do the shopping and visit some of the local beaches. She had even met a few of the local young people and had spent one or two evenings at the local surfers' bar, enjoying the live music on offer. But she was happiest spending time with her aunt and looking after the four much-loved dogs. She thoroughly enjoyed her long walks with them through the lovely coastal countryside and Jess decided that, for a holiday job, this was pretty good.

When her time in Cornwall had come to an end, Auntie May had been very generous and sent Jess home with a large cheque.

* ★ ★

All that had been seven years ago, and apart from the occasional visit, the family had seen little of Auntie May since. The news of her demise came as a sadness to them all.

'She must have been nearly ninety,' Jess's mother said.

'It's hard to believe that,' Jess countered. 'She had such a love of life and a huge sense of fun.'

'Well, dear, are you going to see what your legacy is? I can't bear the suspense any longer.'

Jess unfolded the thick papers and together she and her mother tried to make sense of the legal phrases.

'It almost looks as if . . . ' Jess began.

' . . . as if she's left you the house,' her mother finished. 'Oh Jess, how wonderful! And how generous.'

'Is that right, though? I mean, is that what all this stuff means?'

'I think so, darling. Isn't that fantastic?'

'But why me? Hasn't she got any other relations?'

'Evidently not. Dad might know, I suppose, but I haven't heard of any. She clearly became fond of you when you stayed with her.'

'I was certainly fond of her,' Jess said, 'but now I feel desperately guilty that I didn't go to see her again after that summer.

'How kind of her to remember me so generously. It's such a beautiful cottage, too. And I suppose I could look for a job in Cornwall. They must need teachers there, mustn't they?'

'But would you want to live so far away from us?' her mother said.

'Mum, I'm twenty-six. If I could have afforded a house, I'd have moved out long ago.' She saw her mother's face fall. 'Sorry, I didn't mean to sound ungrateful. It's just that I'd like some space of my own and I'm sure you and Dad would like some time to yourselves. Heavens, you were married and nearly having a baby by the time you were my age.'

'I suppose so. But I'd miss you terribly.'

'You could come down for holidays. Anyway, who says I'm going to live there for sure? I'd have to teach another term here, whatever happens. But it does give me a purpose for the holidays, doesn't it? So how do you fancy a trip to Cornwall?'

'We've already promised Kim we'll go and stay with her and Joe for a week or so. We'll have to see later on. But Jess, dear, you have no idea what state the cottage is in. It could be uninhabitable.'

'You don't think the legacy includes the dogs, do you?'

'Read through the rest of the jargon and see if it says anything about the dogs. But they're probably not around any more. It's a long time since you were there.'

★ ★ ★

Once the idea of owning Auntie May's cottage had sunk in, Jess felt more and more excited at the prospect. Her mind raced through all sorts of possibilities. She could hand in her notice at school at the start of term and possibly leave at half term, in the Autumn. Or maybe she should stay on till Christmas? If she continued to save up till then, she could take some time off to look for another job and work on the cottage. But nothing could be decided till she had been down to look at the place . . . her place . . . and see what needed to be done.

★ ★ ★

Three days later, Jess packed up her car and set off on the long drive to Cornwall. She had made an appointment to see the solicitors in Penzance, to sign some papers and collect the keys to her aunt's cottage.

'I was very surprised to receive this legacy,' she confided to the elderly solicitor. 'I mean, didn't Auntie May have any closer relations?'

'Your aunt was very fond of you,

Miss Cunningham, and seemed grateful for the time you had spent with her. I did mention her sister's children when she made her will, but she was quite emphatic about not having anything to do with them.'

'I didn't even know she had a sister. Dad never mentioned anyone else in the family,' Jess said in surprise, making a mental note to ask about this sister when she next spoke to her father.

'I believe there was some rift many years ago.'

'And this sister had children?' Jess asked.

'So I believe. But, in accordance with your aunt's wishes, you have inherited her cottage. There are a few charity bequests to be completed and there should also be some cash to come. I can't give you the amount at this time, but it will be enough to help you settle in.'

'What happened to the dogs?' Jess wanted to know.

'I'm afraid they had come to the end of their time. May's last months were spent without her beloved rescue dogs. Walking them became too much for her and so she didn't replace them as they gradually left her.'

'How sad. I wish I'd known, but she never said much in her letters.'

After her business with the solicitor was concluded, Jess drove to the cottage where she had been so happy in that far-off summer.

★ ★ ★

The place smelt neglected. Damp and musty. She opened the windows to let in the bright sunlight and wandered round. Strange to see the familiar place without the enthusiastic, friendly dogs. It felt somehow intrusive to be here on her own, but she supposed she would get used to the idea that the place was now hers. She would have to do a great deal of sorting out. In fact, looking around, there was going to be a lot of work needed to make the place more comfortable.

She went into the bathroom and sniffed. A most unpleasant smell greeted her. Blocked drains? Whatever it was, she would need someone more expert than her to come and take a look.

She wandered round the rest of the house and soon had a long list of tasks that needed either her, or some expert help, to sort out.

She glanced at her watch and realised it was already getting late. She still needed to organise somewhere to sleep and get a meal of some kind. Not knowing if there was bedding available, she had brought a sleeping bag. In view of the dampness everywhere, she decided she would sleep on the sofa tonight and sort out her bedroom the next day. As for food, she could always go to the village and see what the pub had to offer. Apart from anything else, she could make sure that people knew she was living at her aunt's house now.

She opened the fridge to put away the few things her mother had insisted she bring to 'start her off'. She quickly closed it again. It had been left for too long and mould was growing everywhere. She added, sort fridge, to her long list of things to be done.

Feeling suddenly overwhelmed by the size of the task ahead, Jess decided she really needed to seek some company and set off for the village pub.

★ ★ ★

The pub was empty when Jess arrived and she ordered her meal and a glass of dry white wine.

'You here on holiday?' the friendly barman asked.

'I've come down to my aunt's cottage. Well, my cottage now,' Jess told him. 'Did you know May Cunningham?'

'Elderly lady. Had a load of dogs?'

'That's right.'

'Think we all knew her. Quite a character. Heard she'd passed on. I'm sorry. Are you planning to live here, then?'

'I don't know yet. Maybe. Depends on whether I can get a job here.'

They chatted on until Jess's meal was ready. Several other people had come into the pub, and judging by the surreptitious looks Jess was getting, the news of her arrival was spreading.

A couple came to sit at the next table and the questions began. Jess related her concerns about all the work that needed done on the cottage.

'What you need is my brother Jack to come round and sort you out. He'll do your drains and any other building jobs you have. Shall I get him to give you a call?' the man said.

'That's very kind,' Jess replied. 'If you give me your brother's name and number, I can certainly get him to give me a quote.'

The woman scribbled something on a piece of paper.

'You'll need to ask him soon, as he's a busy man,' she said. 'Might not be able to fit you in later in the year.'

'Thanks anyway,' Jess said. 'Now, if

you'll excuse me, I must get back.'

Dusk was falling as Jess walked back along the quiet lane. She felt no qualms about being out alone in such a quiet spot and enjoyed the scent of the late flowering honeysuckle in the hedgerows. There were certainly much worse places to live, she mused.

The sky was a pale azure blue in the rapidly fading light, with still a hint of orange tinging the clouds to the far west. She breathed deeply with a small sigh of contentment and made up her mind there and then. She would definitely look for a job down here.

She had been teaching in her present school for three years now and it was probably time for a change. Schools always wanted science teachers, even junior ones, so there might be something available down here.

She let herself into the quiet cottage and once more opened the windows. A good clean through would soon help make the place smell fresher.

Despite feeling very tired, Jess slept

fitfully. The unfamiliar surroundings and the quietness kept her awake. There were no street lamps shining through the curtains, and everywhere was pitch black. She found herself straining to hear every sound and she even imagined she heard someone moving around outside. She rebuked herself. There could be nobody around in such a quiet lane. It led nowhere but to her cottage and petered out into little more than a track.

Jess rose early, showered and made herself breakfast. The milk she had brought with her was off and she threw it down the sink. Black coffee and toast seemed the best she could do.

She sat in the sun on the back step and made her plans for the day. Several loads of washing should be the start, always assuming the washing machine worked. Cleaning the fridge came next, and she would need to do some shopping very soon.

She swallowed the bitter coffee and went back inside. She stripped sheets and blankets off all the beds and brought them down to be washed. Fortunately, it was a bright morning with a brisk drying breeze. With all the windows open, the musty smell of the place was disappearing fast. She put the radio on and music filled the air. She hummed as she worked, collecting more and more heaps of washing in the tiny kitchen.

She took the first load out to the washing line strung between the trees in the pretty, but neglected, garden. More work, Jess thought. She had never done any gardening herself. Her father took pride and joy in their own plot at home and never allowed anyone to tug out so much as a single weed. Not that she knew what were weeds and what were prize plants. Maybe her parents would come down and help her.

'Hello,' called a voice from the lane. Jess swung round and crossed to the gate.

'Hello,' she replied to the good-looking young man standing by a 4×4.

'Can I help you?'

'I'm Dan Meadows. I was checking on Miss Cunningham's place. I live at the farm that backs on to the cottage. I've been keeping an eye on the place and I heard music. I wanted to be sure there weren't squatters moving in.'

Jess smiled. 'Well, I can assure you I'm no squatter. I'm Jessica Cunningham. Jess to most people. I rarely reply if I'm called Jessica.'

'I suppose in that case I'm Daniel and rarely reply unless I'm called Dan. So are you thinking of buying this place?'

'My Aunt May has left it to me. I'm down here to see what needs to be done. Washing, washing and more washing at the moment! I'd ask you in for a coffee, but I haven't any milk and the whole place is in chaos.'

'Not to worry. I just wanted to be sure all was well.'

The young man gave a wave and got back into his car. Jess smiled and waved back as he drove down the track.

She gave an appreciative smile as he disappeared from view. His dark hair and blue eyes had certainly made an impression. About thirty maybe? Tall and tanned. Very nice. Looked as if he was used to outdoor work and probably enjoyed sport as well. He could be a definite asset to the scenery.

On the other hand, he was probably married with a couple of kids and several dogs.

She gave a giggle. What was she like? One good-looking man and her imagination was running riot. No doubt Mrs Dan Meadows would be round with a pot of homemade jam and a sponge cake at any moment.

★ ★ ★

It was almost one o'clock by the time Jess had finished the first batch of her chores. She decided she had better go and do some shopping. At least the fridge was now clean enough to put food in.

She drove to the nearby town, loaded a trolley in the supermarket, and went out to the car. She sniffed the air. Somewhere close by they were baking Cornish pasties. Her stomach rumbled and she knew she just had to have one.

She bought a pastie and sat in the car park to eat it. It was heaven. Tender meat and fluffy potato, with onions and turnip.

As she was in the middle of eating, she saw a shadow fall across her window and looked up. It was Dan Meadows. She wound the window down.

'You enjoyed that didn't you?' he grinned.

Jess felt mortified that Dan had caught her in the act of scoffing a Cornish pasty in the car.

'I . . . well . . . I was starving and had nothing to eat at home,' she said lamely.

Dan laughed. 'It's OK, I have been known to eat Cornish pasties myself.'

He paused and then said tentatively, 'Actually, I was going to ask if you'd maybe like to go out for a drink this evening? Maybe have a bite to eat? If you've any room left after one of Joan's pasties!'

Jess hesitated. She had only met Dan Meadows once, and now here he was asking her to go out with him.

She knew nothing about him. But then again, she knew no-one down here, and she did rather fancy an evening out in the company of a good-looking man. And if they went for a meal, she wouldn't actually be alone with him, would she?

He was looking at her hopefully and rather shyly.

She made up her mind.

'That's very kind,' she said. 'I'd love a drink and I'm sure I'll be ready for something else to eat by this evening.'

'That's great! I'll pick you up around half seven.'

'Thank you. That will be lovely.' She smiled as Dan turned away, collected a trolley and disappeared into the store.

Jess ate the last of her pasty and started the car.

Maybe life in the country wasn't going to be so bad after all.

Making Friends

For the rest of the afternoon, Jess continued her grand clear-out. By six o'clock she felt exhausted, grubby and desperate for a cup of tea. There were still a couple of loads of washing waiting for her to do tomorrow, along with several piles of ironing. Her mobile phone rang. It was her mother.

'Jess? How are you? You never let us know you'd arrived safely. We've been so worried.'

'I'm sorry Mum, it's all been rather hectic. The place is in a bit of a mess and I've been trying to clear it up. But don't worry, everything's fine.'

'Well, if you say so. I hope you're eating properly.'

'Of course I am. I had a wonderful Cornish pasty at lunch and I'm eating out this evening.'

'Oh, really? Where are you going?'

'Just to the pub.' Jess bit her tongue. If she mentioned Dan, it would lead to a whole raft of questions. Fortunately, her mother didn't pursue her interest in Jess's plans for the evening. Instead, she just said, 'That's nice, dear. And remember, do let us know if there's anything you need.'

'I could do with Dad's expertise in the garden,' Jess confessed. 'It's a bit of a mess and I don't know a weed from a chrysanthemum.'

'Well, we'll have to see later on. Look, I'd better go now. Your sister's got supper on the table. Bye dear. Look after yourself.'

'Bye, Mum.'

★　★　★

Jess's thoughts strayed to her sister, Kim. Four years older than Jess, Kim always seemed to do everything right. She'd married her first boyfriend and to their parents' delight, produced two perfect children.

She thought about Dan. Did he have brothers and sisters? What were his likes and dislikes? It was such an interesting time, she thought, meeting someone new and learning about them. She smiled happily and went for a shower, before putting on her favourite blouse and a fashionable pair of trousers. She brushed her long blonde hair and caught it back into a clip.

She peered at herself critically in the mirror. Maybe it was time to get her hair cut. She was getting a bit old for the long, straight-haired blonde look.

Jess put on the minimum of make up and then went downstairs to check that all the windows were closed. However remote this cottage was, it seemed only sensible to take the usual security precautions.

It was seven-fifteen. Quarter of an hour to go before seeing Dan.

She decided she would take off the loose covers tomorrow and wash them.

There was still a whiff of elderly dog about them. Maybe she would be able to afford a new sofa and an easy chair or two. Auntie May's were pretty ancient and took up a lot of space in the living-room. There were some nice antique pieces with which she would never part, but some things would have to go.

'Sorry Auntie May,' she whispered, 'it isn't that I'm not grateful, but some things just need changing.' The old clock ticked its response, a comforting, familiar sound in the room.

Jess heard a car pull up. She locked the front door and walked down the path towards Dan.

'You're very prompt,' she said with a smile.

'Naturally. It's not every night I get to take out the newest, most glamorous addition to our social circle. And if it's OK with you, I've booked a table in the dining room at the local. Thought you might like to meet some of the folks who live around and about.'

★ ★ ★

It was a pleasant evening. Gradually they found out more about each other and shared some of their likes and dislikes. Dan didn't have a girlfriend, Jess discovered. She also learnt that he had more or less taken over the day-to-day running of their family farm, but his father still saw himself as being in charge. His mother did all the household chores and still treated him as if he was a child, he told Jess with a grimace.

'It gets very frustrating at times. Especially if I want to make any changes or try something new. But, I suppose at thirty-two, I'm in a position most young farmers would envy. The prospect of my own farm in the future is something rare these days. I suppose that's why I put up with living at home.'

'Thirty-two,' Jess murmured. 'I was two years out.'

'I'm sorry?'

'I'd guessed at thirty,' she replied,

blushing slightly.

He laughed. 'And I guessed at . . . what . . . twenty-five?'

'Twenty-six,' she corrected him.

'So we both look younger than our years,' Dan said with a grin.

'Actually,' Jess went on, 'I was thinking I should get my hair cut. Make me look less like an aging teenager.'

'Don't you dare. It's beautiful hair.'

She blushed again.

'And why would anyone want to look older?' Dan said.

'Oh, you know. Teaching. Get more respect from the kids.' She smiled. 'Why did I never meet you when I came to look after Auntie May? That was about six years ago.'

'I'd have been abroad then. I did a course in agriculture and then went to New Zealand for a year.'

'Oh, how fantastic!' Jess enthused. 'What was it like?'

'It was hard work and I was doing crazy hours, so I didn't get to see all that much of the country.'

'I was a young student in those days. I did hang out a bit with some of the surfer crowd when I was down here, but mainly I was here to work. Well, I say work, but it was a pleasure, actually.'

They chatted easily, laughed a lot and gave each the impression they were thoroughly enjoying the evening.

At ten o'clock, Jess gave a yawn. 'I'm so sorry. I'm just exhausted. I didn't sleep much last night and I've been working hard all day.'

'Don't worry about it. I always have an early start myself. So if you're finished, I'll take you home now.'

'Thanks, Dan. It's been a lovely evening. I really enjoyed it.'

Jess looked at him shyly. 'I could return the favour, if you wanted.'

'Are you offering to cook for me?'

'I was thinking more of buying fish and chips and we could eat them on the beach,' she laughed.

'I might just take you up on that! Now, shall we make a move?'

★ ★ ★

They drove down the lane and Dan stopped outside Jess's gate. All the windows were brightly lit. 'Funny. I didn't think I'd left any lights on,' Jess said anxiously. 'But I suppose I must have done. Anyway, thank you again. It's been a lovely evening.'

'Whoa there, I'm not letting you go inside on your own. If you didn't leave the lights on, someone might have broken in.'

Jess was worried now. And she was sure she had turned all the lights off when she left.

She turned to Dan gratefully. 'It would be comforting to have you with me. Just in case.'

They walked up the path and Jess unlocked the door. She heard music playing and turned anxiously to look at Dan. 'I certainly didn't leave the radio on.'

'Stay here. I'll take a look around.' He pushed open the kitchen door.

'Nobody in here. I'll look upstairs, if that's okay.'

'I'd be grateful if you would. I'll come with you.' They went up the narrow stairs and Dan opened the various doors, even peering into cupboards and under the beds. Nothing. No sign of any intrusion at all.

'Looks as if I must have left the radio on after all,' Jess said. 'Although I'm sure I didn't. Still, I was feeling a bit tired . . .'

'You will take care, won't you?' Dan said. 'Maybe you need to get the electrics checked out.'

'Yes, you're right. I'll do that. Now, as a thanks for your help, can I make you a coffee?'

'That would be nice, thanks.'

Jess went into the kitchen and reached for the kettle. It was warm.

She looked anxiously at Dan.

'Now I am concerned. The kettle's warm and there's no way I could have left that on.' She looked in the cupboard for mugs and took out two.

One was still wet. There was a spoon in the sink, also still wet. She took the milk out of the fridge. 'That's it. There's a tiny bit taken out of the bottle. Enough for just one cup. Now I know someone has definitely been in here and made themselves a cup of coffee. Who would do that? No-one just goes into a house when the owners are out and helps themselves to coffee.'

'Do you want me to call the police for you?' Dan asked.

'I can hardly tell them someone came in and stole a cup of coffee,' Jess replied, spooning coffee powder into the mugs and stirring vigorously. 'There was nothing else missing and besides, everything was still locked up, wasn't it? No windows open or broken. Not exactly a break-in.'

'Look, if you'd rather not stay here alone tonight, I'm sure Mum wouldn't mind you staying over at our place.'

'That's very kind of you, but I'll be fine. I could have left the switches on, as I said.'

'I might have agreed, except for the kettle and the wet coffee mug. Has anyone else got a key?'

'I don't think so. But maybe May left a key with a neighbour or something. Maybe they didn't realise I'd moved in.'

'Hang on a minute. When I was staying here, May always left a key outside in case she got locked out. I bet it's still there. And any number of people would have known about that.'

'Let's go and look. And you'd probably better make sure it isn't left out again. I bet you're right though, and that's all it was. Someone has been used to dropping in and having a coffee with May.'

★　★　★

They went out to the garden and Jess looked round for the planter where May used to leave her key. It was still there. A long, terracotta trough, once filled with geraniums but now just a collection of dried weeds. She lifted one

32

corner and there was the key. She could see it had been recently moved.

'I suggest you take that key inside,' Dan told her. 'If you really need a key left somewhere, find a new place, more secure and don't tell anyone about it.'

'You're right. I'll take it inside now.'

'Are you sure you're happy to stay here? I can still give Mum a ring, you know.'

Jess smiled at Dan. 'I'm fine. I'm sure there's a simple explanation and it was some old friend of Auntie May who's used to coming and going through the house. Doubtless I'll meet them at some point. Thanks again for a lovely evening and for coming to my rescue!'

'All right then, if you're sure.' Dan leaned towards her and gave her a peck on the cheek. She smiled as he gently touched her arm. She liked this man. Really liked him.

She waved him off and went back inside. Despite her brave words about feeling safe, she went round the house again and checked that every window was firmly shut and that the front and back doors were locked. Whoever her intruder was, they must have been aware of the changes she had made, Jess thought. Fresh milk in the fridge and the massive basket of ironing was a dead giveaway. She checked the doors yet again before going up to bed, where she sank gratefully into her clean, fresh sheets and feel asleep instantly.

Around six-thirty next morning, she woke to hear a strange noise. She tensed and lay still for a minute or two, trying to identify the sound. Cats? Sea birds? Some small creature in the garden? Whatever it was, it had succeeded in thoroughly waking her. Well, she certainly had plenty to do, so an early start wasn't a bad thing.

Wondering if she was becoming paranoid, she made another inspection of the cottage to make sure nobody had come in while she had been asleep.

She peered out of the little windows but could see nothing to help identify the strange noises. Maybe she should get a dog, she thought. The cottage was used to them and it would help make her feel safe. But then she realised that would be making a firm commitment to living here. Clearly, she needed to plan her future properly and not make any rash decisions about dogs or anything else. She doubted that even Auntie May's promised cash legacy would be much to live on for very long. And she still had her teaching job to go back to, with notice to serve, even if she did decide to leave.

Feeling more confident in the daylight, Jess opened the windows to let the fresh air fill the house and gave a wry smile at the thought of her anxiety the night before.

She made some breakfast and sat outside in the warm sunshine. She planned her day and wondered what she could do with her time once the spring clean was over.

There were lots of things she wanted to try. All manner of crafts and possibly painting. She had loved art at school but had chosen to take science subjects. But whatever she did, Jess knew that teaching would always be her first love and anyway, she needed to work to earn money.

Curtains, she told herself, coming back down to earth. Must wash the curtains and the windows.

It was around midday when she was washing the upper floor windows on the inside and wondering how she would ever reach them from the outside, that she saw Dan's car pull up. He waved and she came down to greet him.

'Just wanted to check you were okay. No more intruders?' he asked.

'No, I'm fine. Can I offer you some coffee or something?'

'If you've got the time I'm on my way to the farm suppliers. I need some fencing to keep Mum's wretched goats in. Honestly, they're such a pain and they're always escaping.'

'Did they get out in the night? Well, early this morning?'

'Oh dear. You heard them?'

'Yes, I'm sure it must have been them. They gave me a bit of a fright, but I think I was a bit jumpy anyway after last night.'

'I'm sorry they scared you. And by the way, I asked Mum if she knew of anyone who might have come round, and she couldn't think of anyone. She said May hardly ever had any visitors. I think she got on with Mum all right, but she was always very independent. Never wanted to be a nuisance to anyone. You should call round and see Mum when you've got time. She'd be delighted to have a gossip and a chat about May.'

'Thanks, I will,' Jess said. 'Once I've got my spring cleaning done. I'm getting quite obsessed with it! Anyway, I'll go and put the kettle on.'

They sat in the garden to drink their coffee. 'I guess this will be the next big chore. I hate gardening,' Jess said, looking out over the unkempt lawn and overgrown flower beds. 'No, actually,' she went on, 'it's not true that I hate gardening. The truth is that I've never actually done any. My dad never let anyone near his precious plants.'

'I could come and give you a hand,' Dan offered. 'I don't claim to know much about it, but I could certainly help with grass cutting and cutting back bushes.'

'That's very kind of you. But I really couldn't accept.' She knew she couldn't offer to pay him and it seemed such a daunting task.

'Oh come on, it might be fun,' Dan said. 'We could do it together.'

'Well, when you put it like that, it's very generous of you. Thank you. You might even be able to stop me from pulling up some exotic plant that should be cherished and nurtured.'

'I think we'll need to get through the weeds of ages first. I don't suppose anything's been done to the garden for a long time. May could hardly manage much more than a bit of light weeding in her latter months.'

'Poor May. I really should have

visited her more often. Did you ever see anything of any other relations?'

'Like I said, you'd need to speak to Mum. Why don't you come round for supper this evening and meet her?'

Jess looked alarmed. 'Oh, I couldn't. Not just like that.'

'Nonsense. I'm inviting you. And she's dying to meet you. After we went out last night, she's been pumping me ever since. You'd certainly get a decent meal. What do you say?'

'Well, only if she doesn't mind. You must ask her first and I won't be offended if she prefers to make it some other time.'

'I assume you have a mobile? Give me the number and I'll get her to call you. Will that do?'

'Okay. Thanks. I haven't bothered to get the phone reconnected here. I don't know how long I'll be staying and it's not worth paying for something I might never use.'

Jess gave Dan her mobile number and he tapped it into his own phone.

'I'll get her to call you later. I'd better go now or she'll wonder who's been spiriting me away from my chores. I'll tell her those wretched goats kept you awake and that'll make her feel guilty and she'll feel she has to cook you a sumptuous meal.'

'Don't you dare say anything of the sort! Go and buy your barbed wire or whatever it is you need.'

'You don't know much about the countryside, do you? Barbed wire? To keep goats in? I don't think so. Stock netting. High spec stock netting. They'll eat through anything, those guys.'

'Whatever. Go on then, and let me get back to my washing.'

Jess watched Dan leave, realising her feelings for him were growing.

'Stop trying to rush things,' she scolded herself. But there were only five weeks left of her holidays.

A Mysterious Letter

All Jess's efforts to get rid of the unidentified smell in her bathroom had come to nothing. Clearly, she needed expert help. She thought of calling Jack, the man whose sister had recommended him when she'd gone to the pub that first evening, but something made her hold back. She would wait and see if Dan's parents knew of anyone reliable, or if indeed, Jack was a suitable person to ask. Mind you, Mrs Meadows hadn't called yet, she reminded herself. Perhaps it wasn't convenient for her to have an uninvited guest that evening.

She went into Auntie May's old room. The bed was stripped and the clean curtains were waiting to be hung. Most of May's clothes and personal bits and pieces had been taken away. She remembered a clause in the Will that had left them to some charity and assumed the solicitor had arranged all that. It was quite a relief not to have to deal with such personal things.

There were, however, several of May's boxes that she needed to look through, although it seemed intrusive to look through someone's things, even if they were now officially hers.

She opened the first box. It contained several pieces of costume jewellery. Old-fashioned brooches and several sets of beads. There was also a little box holding a beautiful silver bangle. It was inscribed: *To my Darling May. My love always, Derek.*

'Well, well,' Jess murmured, 'so who was Derek?'

Maybe this was a question her father might answer. It was his family, after all.

There was little of any great value in the box but she fingered some of the beads, remembering her aunt wearing them. They would be put away safely and kept along with many memories.

The next box Jess opened was larger. Inside, she found a number of old papers and photographs. There was also a yellowed newspaper cutting. She unfolded it carefully and stared at the faint print and the blurred photograph of a man and woman in wedding dress.

The wedding of Miss June Cunningham (20) and Mr Derek Wishart (29) took place at Cove Church, near Penzance, last Saturday. The bride was attended by her cousin, Miss Daisy Williams. The best man was Mr Phillip Wishart, brother of the groom. Following a reception at the bride's home, the couple left for a honeymoon in Devon.

There was no year given, but from the look of the clothes it was after the war. Late forties, perhaps? Derek. She remembered the silver bangle and its inscription. Was Derek the reason the two sisters had fallen out? May hadn't been a bridesmaid at her own sister's wedding.

Jess had a sudden thought. Her gran was called Daisy. Whether or not she was a Miss Williams before her marriage, she had no idea, but surely her father would know that. Something else to ask him.

She looked into the box again. There was a bundle of letters, two of which had never been opened. What a dilemma. Should she look to see who they were from?

While she was debating with herself, her mobile rang. It was Dan's mother, inviting her to supper that evening.

'I'd love to come,' Jess said, 'but I don't want you to feel you have to invite me for a meal, Mrs Meadows. Wouldn't you rather I just called in for a cup of tea or something?'

'Of course not, dear. If Dan has invited you, we'd be delighted to see you. About six-thirty?'

'Thank you very much. I'd love to meet you. And I have lots of questions for you about my aunt.'

'I hope I'll be able to answer some of

them. I look forward to seeing you later.'

'Thank you.'

Dan's mother sounded nice. Really friendly.

* * *

Jess went back to her search. The writing on one of the unopened envelopes was neat and probably written by a female. The postmark was blurred but it looked as if it was written in nineteen fifty something. The other unopened envelope was clearly marked as nineteen fifty-four. Jess put them to one side. She looked further into the box and found a collection of old birthday cards and several hand-written receipts for furniture, probably the same three piece suite that was presently in the lounge.

The two unopened letters remained beside her, on the bed. She took a deep breath and ripped the oldest one open first.

'Dear May,

I know you will never forgive me for what I did. I'm sorry, but I couldn't help falling in love with Derek. Perhaps I shouldn't have married him, but there it is. Anyway, I wanted to be the one to tell you that I'm expecting. The baby's due in April. Should I continue the family tradition and call her April, if it's a girl? Please write back to tell me I am forgiven.

Your loving sister, June.'

It was quite clear that May hadn't written back and nor had she forgiven her sister. She hadn't even opened her letter.

The second letter was also from June.

'Dear May,

I was sorry you couldn't see fit to reply to my last letter. After all these years, isn't it time we buried the hatchet? My daughter is now three and I am pleased to say that I am again expecting. I'd very much like to see you and introduce you to your niece. I hope you are happy now that the cottage is yours. I suppose I can understand why our parents left it to you. Some sort of compensation perhaps. Derek and I have a nice rented home, so I suppose I shouldn't grumble. I do miss you, especially now our parents are gone. Please write back.

Your loving sister, June.

P.S. Our little girl is called April and she looks just like you.'

Jess laid the letters down and sat staring across the room. Poor May. She had lost the love of her life, her sister and her parents. The cottage must have been some compensation to her, but she had remained bitter enough to leave her sister's letters unopened for the rest of her life.

What had happened to June and Derek Wishart? What about their daughter and the second child? She must phone her father and see if he knew anything about them. Maybe the solicitor might know something. It would be worth contacting him, Jess thought.

Dan's' parents, Mr and Mrs Meadows, were a jolly pair. They clearly enjoyed life, especially now that Dan had taken over the bulk of the work of running the farm. They made her feel very welcome. Mrs Meadows was small and motherly, while her husband was almost as tall as his son and had the same startlingly blue eyes.

Mrs Meadows was an excellent cook and served a hearty meal of roast lamb and wonderful fresh vegetables. The plum pie for dessert was made with fruit from their own trees and even the cream came from their own cows.

'That was an amazing meal. Thank you so much. I wish I could cook like that. And I suppose you grow all your own vegetables too?' Jess said.

'Certainly do,' Mr Meadows said proudly. 'None of your supermarket rubbish for us.'

'Shall I help you clear, Mrs Meadows?' Jess asked.

'You're our guest, Jess. You just sit there.'

'No, really, I'd like to help,' Jess insisted and picked up some of the serving dishes.

'I've got a dishwasher so just leave them on the side,' Mrs Meadows said. 'Now, didn't you want to ask me something about your aunt?'

'I've been trying to find out about her sister, and her sister's children.'

'I never heard tell of anyone else in her family,' Mrs Meadows said. 'I certainly remember you coming down to help out a few years back, when the old lady took a tumble. There was nobody else to help her from what I could gather. I think you came to stay when you were a little 'un as well. With your mum and dad. And you had a sister, didn't you?'

'Yes, Kim. She's married now and has two little boys. My parents are staying with her at the moment. They usually go and spend a week or two during the holidays.'

'Well now, let me think. A sister to May. Don't think I ever knew anything about her.'

'She was called June,' Jess said. 'She married a Derek Wishart. In the late forties, I'd guess.'

'There used to be some Wisharts down Penzance way. He played cricket for the County at one time, I think. Mind you, I'm going back a few years.'

They chatted for some time and though the names mentioned were familiar, Mrs Meadows couldn't add much to the information Jess already had. Nor could she shed any light on the mystery visitor the previous evening.

★ ★ ★

The dog lying close to the Aga stretched and stood up. 'She looks like one of Auntie May's old dogs,' Jess remarked.

'Certainly is,' Dan's mother said. 'One of her dogs had a litter of pups.

Lizzie here is a lovely girl.'

The dog thumped its tail and Jess bent to stroke her.

'I was thinking I might get a dog if I decide to move down here permanently,' she said.

'Is that on the cards, then?' Mrs Meadows asked.

'I'm not sure yet. I'd have to work my notice for my teaching job and find another post down here.'

'It would be nice if you did. And I'd hate the idea of May's cottage being just another holiday home. Pretty little place in its day.'

★ ★ ★

When they went into the sitting room, Dan and his father were engrossed in a discussion about milk quotas. Clearly, the argument was not going Dan's way.

'Now you two,' said Mrs Meadows, 'that's enough. It's always the same, Jess. Whenever they're in a room together, they talk shop, and that leads to yet another endless argument.'

'Dad doesn't like to admit he's wrong. Or that things might have changed just a little since Noah landed the Ark,' Dan said.

'All you want to do is to change everything for change's sake. If it ain't broke, don't fix it,' grumbled his father.

'That's enough, you two. What will Jess be thinking of us?' Mrs Meadows was clearly used to keeping her two men in line, and Jess laughed.

'Would you like to take a walk round the farm?' Dan offered.

'Thanks, yes. That would be nice. If you don't mind?' Jess asked his parents.

'Not at all dear, you run along,' Mrs Meadows said. 'I'll make some coffee while you're away.'

★ ★ ★

It was a lovely place, *Long Meadows*. 'Very aptly named,' Jess said, seeing the sign at the end of the drive.

'Always been a bit of a joke around

here,' Dan said. 'We tell Mum it was named for her, the only short Meadows to live here.'

He led her to the milking parlour and she admired the spotless long shed with individual stalls to cope with the large number of cows at milking time. 'They all go straight to their own places and wait. Amazingly clever animals, cows.'

'You love your life don't you?' Jess said. 'You're very lucky to be able to work at something you enjoy so much.'

'Don't you enjoy your life?'

'Yes, of course I do. Well, most of the time.'

Jess admired the neatly kept yard and the sturdy field fences. Fluffy white sheep grazed further up the hillside and there was a hen run with assorted hens scratching the earth.

'They're Mum's hens. She always liked having a few around for the eggs but now they have to be kept in a proper run. New legislation. Just as well, really, as there are several foxes on the land. And through here,' Dan said, pushing open a heavy farm gate, 'are Mum's pesky goats.'

Jess grinned at several pigmy goats standing in a heavily fenced paddock. 'They're so small, I can't believe they're the terrible creatures you described to me,' she said to Dan.

'Believe me, they're monsters. They look cute enough but they can ravage a field in one night. What they can't eat, they trample and jump around in.'

'Well, I think they're lovely. And you seem to have a bit of everything here.'

'I think that's part of the trouble. It's labour intensive and too much variation means some aspects don't make enough profit. But try convincing my dad of that.'

'Both of you do seem to have the farm's interests at heart, even if you disagree about some things.'

'You're a lovely girl Jess,' Dan said suddenly. 'I really hope you will come down here to live.' He took her hand and squeezed her fingers gently. She smiled up at him, feeling her heart beating somewhat faster than usual. He let his arm rest gently on her shoulders and she liked the feel of his warmth.

He said softly, 'Am I allowed to kiss you?'

'I'd like that,' she replied. And so he did.

The pigmy goats bleated as if in protest and they both laughed as they broke apart.

★ ★ ★

Dan insisted on walking back to Jess's cottage with her to make sure all was well.

He kissed her as he left and promised to give her a call very soon. 'And make sure you lock up properly,' he called from the gate.

She grinned and waved. It was rather nice having someone to care.

Tired though she was, once inside, Jess sat down and began to make some notes. She was making discoveries about her family and wanted to be sure she remembered everything. When she had more details, she would talk to her father and see what he could remember. He had never mentioned anyone other than Auntie May on his side of the family. It was all very intriguing.

She gave a yawn and knew that trying to do anything more was pointless. Besides, there were many more letters in May's boxes, and contained in those letters was possibly a whole family history, just waiting to be discovered.

★　★　★

The endless washing and ironing, cleaning and tidying seemed to take up most of Jess's time. But she felt she was making progress and her lists of things which needed replaced or which needed outside help, were growing. She spoke to her mother a few times but kept her search into the family history to herself. She planned to go to the library to see if she could look at their old records and track down any of the Wishart family. She knew the name and approximate date of birth of one of the children. Children. They must be well into their fifties by now and probably had children of their own. There were still several more packages in the precious boxes and she was saving the possibility of more discoveries until she had finished the chores she had set herself. That time was now coming, but first she needed to get a plumber in to see what was wrong in the bathroom.

Perhaps Dan might know of a plumber. She had forgotten to ask when she'd been to visit the farm. She phoned his mobile.

'Hi there,' he said cheerfully. The noises surrounding him suggested he was in the middle of a flock of sheep. 'Nice to hear from you, but can I call you back in a few minutes?'

'Yes, of course.'

She switched off her phone and waited for a few minutes, wondering what to do next. Maybe she should call Jack, the brother of the woman she'd met in the pub. But she had no idea who he was and if he was reliable.

She decided to wait until Dan called back.

It was half an hour before he returned her call.

'Sorry. Minor crisis with a sheep trapped in some wire. Had to cut it out and then repair the gap. Stupid animals at times. Now, what can I do for you? Are you inviting me for that fish and chip picnic?'

'I wasn't actually, though if you'd like that, I'm up for it. No, I was going to ask you if you knew a tame plumber. Someone called Jack was recommended.'

'Oh no. Forget him. Bit of a cowboy. Try Mr Tranter in the village. He's very good. Not particularly quick, but he does a good job. You got problems?'

'I'm not really sure. There's a horrible smell in the bathroom that bleach or any other cleaner known to mankind seems unable to shift.'

'Well, I'd definitely recommend Mr

Tranter. He's done work for us and I think your aunt had him round, too. I've got his number back in the house. I'll bring it round to you when I come for my picnic.'

'What? Tonight?'

'Yes, tonight. I'll be round about seven, then we can drive to the chip shop.'

★   ★   ★

Jess wandered out into the garden. This also needed some fairly massive work. She remembered the old shed at one end of the path and fought her way through brambles, nettles and green things that had once been plants. She tugged at the door to open the shed and saw there was a whole collection of tools, including an electric mower. Maybe she could at least cut the lawn.

She jumped as a sound came from the back of the shed. Suspecting a rat, she backed out, calling an ineffective *shoo* as she went. There was another sound, this time more recognisable. It was a cat.

'Hello?' she called softly. 'Come here, puss.' There was a clatter as plastic plant pots toppled from an unsteady pile and a small black and white cat emerged, shaking itself. 'Hello you,' Jess said softly. 'Where have you come from?' The cat went back inside the shed and came out a couple of minutes later with something in its mouth. It dropped it near Jess's feet and to her surprise, having initially feared the worst kind of cat present, she realised it was a little kitten.

The tiny creature squeaked as the mother disappeared and returned with a second kitten. In total, five of them were brought out and the cat rubbed itself against Jess. She bent down to stroke it. It was painfully thin.

She found a box and put an old pillow into it and the cat sat in it, deciding whether or not it made a good nest. Approval gained, she collected her family and gently deposited them into the box one by one. Jess smiled and went inside to see what she had that would be suitable for feeding her new family. She poured milk into a dish and opened a can of tuna, which she placed at the side of the box. The cat ate hungrily, then sat and washed itself. It settled down in the makeshift bed and the kittens immediately settled down to feed. Jess watched, enchanted by the way the little mother took care of her babies.

She settled them into her kitchen. She needed to get supplies. Cat litter and a tray. Proper cat food. Did they make special food for nursing mother cats?

She made a shopping list, shut the cat and kittens in the kitchen and drove to the nearest supermarket. She smiled to herself as she put some extra treats for her new little family into the trolley. She added some ready meals and fruit and vegetables for herself and went towards the check-out. She remembered her evening date with Dan and picked up some wine.

Not knowing what Dan liked, she collected a bottle of white and one of red.

When she got back to the car, it was raining steadily. So much for a beach picnic, she thought.

The gate was open when she returned and she assumed the postman must have called. But there were no letters. She could hear the cat mewing and set out its litter tray. She noticed the outside of the kitchen window was covered in marks and made a mental note to clean it again. Perhaps a drainpipe was leaking and had streaked it with mud.

'Having a house is quite a responsibility, isn't it, cat?' Jess said to her new companion.

She put away the shopping and, seeing the rain had stopped, went outside to clean the window. It was quite a mess, with muddy streaks and fingermarks everywhere. The paintwork was scratched, as if someone had been trying to prise open the latch.

Jess shivered. Someone was certainly showing a bit too much interest in her cottage. Was it someone who knew May? Or just an opportunist looking for something to steal? She wondered if she should call the police, but there was no real damage.

She noticed the shed door was still open and went down the path to shut it. With the discovery of the cat and kittens, she must have forgotten to close it, she reasoned. But as she went down the garden, she saw that one of the flower beds had been cleared. There were several colourful heather plants flowering and now that the weeds had gone, they were clearly visible.

She looked around but could see nothing else out of place.

★ ★ ★

Jess fed the cat again, not sure how much it really needed but as it was so thin, it surely wouldn't do it any harm.

The kittens were all fast asleep in a contented, furry heap, so she let the mother out into the garden. It must have trusted her, she realised, to leave her babies. It was a good feeling.

At seven o'clock prompt, Dan walked up the path. He went to ring the old ship's bell that served as a door bell, but it was missing. He knocked on the door.

'What's happened to your bell?' he said when Jess let him in

'Have you taken it down to clean it?'

'Oh dear,' Jess said. 'Someone must have taken it. I knew someone had been here when I was out this afternoon. Oddly enough, they even did some gardening. Cleared one of the flower beds. It wasn't you, was it? Or your dad? I did wonder if you might have been doing a non-gardener a good turn.'

'It certainly wasn't me,' Dan said, 'and I really think you should call the police. I know you think it's only petty stuff, but they might get more ambitious. What's that noise?' he asked, as he heard the kittens squeaking.

'My new guests. I found them in the shed and brought them in.'

Jess opened the kitchen door. The little cat rubbed itself against her legs and the heap of kittens squeaked in protest at being left.

'You are a tender-hearted soul aren't you? What on earth are you going to do with a cat and four kittens?' Dan said.

'Five. Five kittens. I don't know. Find homes for them?'

'You'll be lucky. Everyone round here has got as many cats as they can manage. No, don't look at me. We can't take another whisker. Now, I'm starving. Are you going to buy me this fish supper you promised?'

Dan Acts Strangely

Jess and Dan sat in the car to eat the delicious, steaming fish and chips. It was beginning to rain even harder and thoughts of a walk along the beach had evaporated.

'Gosh, those were good. I haven't had fish and chips for ages.' Dan grinned at her as he wiped his fingers on a tissue.

'I'm full. I can't finish this lot,' Jess confessed.

'I could always help you out.'

She passed Dan the chips still left in her own paper. 'You must have hollow legs, as my Gran used to say.'

'I work hard. Burn off the calories.'

'Actually, Dan, if you don't mind, I'd like to get back home. I'm sure someone was trying to get in through the kitchen window earlier. There was mud all over the sill and they'd tried to prise the catch open. Probably wanted coffee after doing the gardening.'

'This is getting serious,' Dan warned. 'It's more than some prankster. I really must insist you call the police. You could be in danger if they tried to break in when you're there.'

'It always seems to happen when I'm out. As if whoever it is knows when I'm not there. But there's nowhere anyone could hide to watch my movements.'

'Unless someone knows your car and sees when you go past.'

'But you must know pretty well everyone who lives down my lane. It doesn't even have direct access to the beach, so people don't walk down it.'

'There are holiday lets right up to the main road. Means there are likely to be strangers around. It is August and the holiday season,' Dan pointed out.

Jess pondered this. 'I'm not sure about strangers,' she said. 'I almost get the feeling it's someone who knows the place. They knew where the coffee and mugs were kept. And exactly where the key was hidden.'

* * *

They drove back to Jess's cottage, with Dan still trying to persuade her to go to the police. She was touched by his concern but still said no.

Back at the cottage, she took the wine from the fridge. The cat miaowed and rubbed against her legs. The kittens climbed out of their box and scampered around the floor. Dan stood in the doorway. He took the wine bottle from Jess and held out a hand for the corkscrew. She handed it over with a smile and bent to pick up one of the tiny kittens. It nipped at her with tiny pins of teeth and scratched her hand.

'These are wild cats, Jess,' Dan said. 'They're bred to live outside and fend for themselves. You're asking for trouble trying to keep them inside. By all means feed them and give them a box to sleep in, but you really should keep them outside in your shed. They'll be happier in the long run.'

'I don't know. Suppose something like a fox gets them? I'd never forgive myself.'

'I'm sorry, but in the countryside you have to be realistic. Besides, when you go back home, as you say you must, who'll look after them then? If you've got them housetrained and reliant on you for food, they won't be able to hunt for themselves.'

'I suppose you're right. But the little mother cat is so thin.'

'So feed her till she's stronger. But then you need to let them go. They'll move over to our barns. Keep the rats and mice at bay.'

'If you say so.'

'Well now you've seen sense over that, maybe you'll also see the sense in calling the police.'

'All right, if you insist and as long as they won't think I'm being a panic merchant, I'll call them in the morning.

Now, are you going to nurse that wine all evening or can I have some?'

* * *

They chatted about life in the country, about farming and teaching and shared a few moans about the difficulties of living with parents.

'Our mums always do all the cooking, so we've never really had to learn how to fend for ourselves,' Dan said.

Jess smiled at him. 'I can use the microwave and boil an egg.'

'How ever are you coping here, then? No microwave as far as I can see.'

'That's a point. There certainly was one when I was staying with Auntie May. Maybe it got broken.'

'I think you should make a note of anything that seems to have disappeared.'

'It would be difficult to know if things simply broke and were thrown away. I doubt there was ever a record of

70

the house contents.'

'But it would have been valued before it was handed over to you. There may be an inventory.'

★   ★   ★

Dan left around ten o'clock, anxious to get a decent sleep before he was up for milking at five the next morning.

Jess gave the cat and kittens some more milk and shut the kitchen door. She liked the thought of the little animals under her roof, whatever Dan said about them being wild cats, although there was still the problem of her needing to go back home before the new school term began. Perhaps she ought to take Dan's advice and put the cats outside.

★   ★   ★

Jess phoned the local police in the morning. The constable who came round to the cottage was sympathetic, but not hopeful about finding the person responsible. She filled out a form and he told her she could call again if she was troubled further.

'It would be helpful if you actually caught someone in the process of breaking in,' the policeman said. 'But don't try to be brave. Call us.'

'But whoever it is seems to wait till I've gone out. They seem to know when I'm away from home,' Jess pointed out.

'Bit of a problem that. We just don't have the resources to have someone watch the place. And from what you say, they haven't taken much of value, have they? Just an old bell and a cup of coffee.'

'Well, thanks anyway,' Jess said, cross that she'd even allowed herself to be persuaded to involve the police.

When Dan called to ask how it had gone, she said it had been a waste of time.

'I'll be round later. I've an idea,' he said.

Jess decided to spend more time looking through May's box of memories. She'd got over the feeling of being intrusive and was anxious to discover more about the side of the family whose existence had only recently come to light.

It was fascinating. There were lots of old newspaper cuttings referring to various charity events. May had been active in a number of local charities, most of them predictably concerned with dogs and other animal welfare groups. She had run stalls at some of them and given prizes at others.

Jess opened a long envelope which looked newer than the rest of the papers. Inside it was another newspaper cutting, carefully folded.

'*The death is announced of Mr Derek Wishart of Penzance. He died in his own home after a short illness. He was seventy-two. He leaves a wife, son and daughter and two grandchildren.*' A second cutting detailed the funeral and gave a list of the chief mourners and actually had a date, nineteen-ninety-one.

There was no mention of May attending the funeral. How sad that must have been for her, Jess thought.

It appeared that June had a daughter, April, and a son, Julian. April still had the name Wishart, so presumably had never married. Julian had a wife, Judith, and two children, David and Poppy. They seemed to be taking a break from the family tradition of naming children after months of the year.

Jess now knew she had distant cousins who must be around the same age as she was. David and Poppy. What might they be like? Where did they live?

She heard someone knocking at the door and pushed everything back into the box.

'Hi, I've brought you some security.' Dan was standing on the doorstep clutching a cardboard box. 'I remembered my spare camera and thought that we could connect it to a movement sensor. It will then take a picture of anyone calling at your house. Probably get the few odd cats and dogs as well, but that's no problem.'

'That sounds very clever, even if I don't understand what you're talking about,' Jess said.

'You know about movement sensors in burglar alarms? That they have a little light that sets an alarm off if anyone moves past it? Well, it's like that and I've added a gismo that makes the camera take a picture. Well, it does if it works.'

'I've no idea how you're going to make it work, but go ahead if you think you can,' and Jess watched as Dan connected bits of wire and equipment together.

'These are some bits of an electronics kit I had,' he said. 'I rigged up all sorts of things around the farm. I'm not really sure if this will work,' he admitted, 'but it may be worth a try.'

'I'll make some tea while you're doing that.'

'Thanks. That would be great. Then I must get back to the milking.'

'Never a moment's peace, is there?'

'It's what happens when you have living creatures to look after. Speaking of which, how are the cats?'

'Fine. They've taken over the shed. I took your advice and I'm just putting out the odd dish of food. Hopefully, they'll be old enough to look after themselves when I go home.'

Dan tested his camera. It worked twice, then stopped. 'It always was a long shot,' he said. 'I'll leave it here anyway. It may just decide to work occasionally and who knows, we might be lucky and catch the culprit.'

When Dan had gone, Jess called Mr Tranter in the village to see if he could come and look at the plumbing in her bathroom. He arranged to call *dreckly*, as he put it. She'd heard the phrase many times before in Cornwall and smiled.

She glanced at her watch. It was almost four. On impulse, she decided to drive to Cove Church. She knew roughly where it was, and if she could look at the Parish records, she might get more information about May's family.

* * *

Cove was a delightful little church, built close to the cliffs and overlooking a rocky cove. The door was open and Jess went inside. There was little to see, apart from a visitors' book covering the current year and a couple of photo-copied sheets detailing the history of the place. Perhaps she needed to contact the vicar and make an appoint-ment. She chided herself for not thinking of that. They would hardly leave valuable parish books lying around for anyone to look at.

She made a note of the phone number from the notice board and left the building.

She decided to take a short walk along the little beach and breathed in the smell of the salty air. This was such a good place to live. She had definitely made up her mind. This was where she wanted to be. As soon as she went back to her job, she would hand in her notice and look for something in this area. If she couldn't get a teaching post, she would find something else. Thanks to Auntie May, she now knew where her future lay. If Dan became a part of it, then so much the better, but he was certainly not the only reason for making her decision.

★ ★ ★

When Jess opened her cottage door, all seemed to be exactly as she had left it. Dan had shown her how to check the camera and she pressed the buttons. It did not seem to have taken any pictures, but as he had said at the time, it simply may not have worked. She went into the garden and looked around. That too, seemed exactly as she had left it. She looked for the cat and it ran out when she called. The kittens followed, looking more and more like miniature versions of their mother.

It rubbed against her legs. 'How can you be a wild cat, eh?' Jess murmured. Clearly she was going to have to do something with the little family. Maybe she could put a card in a local shop before she left.

After a couple of days, she decided to call Dan and invite him for supper. He hadn't called her and she had to admit to feeling a little disappointed.

She picked up the phone and put it down again several times. If he'd wanted to see her, surely he would have called her or popped round. Well, nothing ventured, she thought, and dialled his number.

'Hi, Dan. How are you?'

'I'm all right. I thought I must have done something wrong. Offended you in some way.' He sounded curt and Jess frowned.

'Have I missed something? Was I

supposed to do something and I haven't?'

'Well, apart from cutting me dead in town the other day. You turned away when I called you and shot off like something nasty was chasing you. I assumed you didn't want to see me.'

'I haven't a clue what you're talking about,' Jess said.

'It was two mornings ago. I was going to ask if the camera had worked but you rushed away.'

'But I haven't been to town since you put up the camera. You must have mistaken someone else for me.'

'Really?' Dan's voice sounded disbelieving . . . in fact, quite sarcastic. 'So someone else is exactly your size, has exactly the same hair colour and hairstyle and wears jeans just like yours.'

'There must be dozens of females with long blond hair who wear jeans. You must have been mistaken, Dan. Truly, I haven't been out since Tuesday afternoon. That was when I drove down to the little church near Penzance, looking for Parish records. Look, I'm sorry, but I have no idea who it might have been. I'd never cut you dead, as you put it. In fact, I was phoning to ask if you'd like to come for supper this evening. It won't be anything special but it would be a chance to see each other.'

'I'm sorry, but I don't think that's a good idea. I don't see much of a future for us if you're going back home soon. Thanks anyway. Sorry, but I must go. Lots to do.'

'Bye,' Jess murmured as his phone was switched off.

What on earth was all that about? she thought. Sadly, she made some coffee and sat on the doorstep drinking it, deep in thought. Clearly he'd mistaken someone else for her but there was surely no reason to be so upset about it? Why would he make such a big thing about it? She tried to remember what else he had said. *No future for us if you're going back home.* That must mean he was beginning to care for her, as she cared for him.

★ ★ ★

For the rest of the day, Jess went over and over Dan's words and decided that, however foolish she might look, she simply must see him and try to sort things out. Besides, she had already decided to look for a job down here in Cornwall.

Jess decided to go to the pub for supper and walked up the lane, enjoying the sunny evening. If she had stayed at home, she would have kept churning over her conversation with Dan and getting nowhere.

There were a few people in the bar when she reached the pub, but it was still early for the main diners. Suddenly, she didn't feel like eating much and ordered a toasted sandwich. She told herself off, as it was something she could easily have made for herself at home. She sat in a corner and ate quietly and got up to leave as soon as she had finished. She paid her bill and said goodnight to the barman.

'How's it going down your lane?' he asked. 'You getting the place straight?'

'Slowly,' she replied with a polite smile. 'There's a lot to do.'

'And will you be selling it? Or do you plan to move here? We all hope it isn't going to be just another holiday home.'

'Early days yet. I'm thinking seriously about staying, but I have to find a job and then work my notice.'

'Well, we're always looking for good kitchen help.'

'You wouldn't want me in your kitchen,' Jess laughed. 'I'd drive your customers away.'

'Barmaid then. You could work behind the bar. Make a very pleasant addition to the scenery.'

'That's very kind of you, but I'll have to think about it.'

She left, with a few people calling goodnight. It seemed she was becoming known in the village and they were clearly being friendly. It was probably because of Auntie May, who had been well known and liked in the community.

It was getting dark as she walked down the lane. She thought she saw a movement behind a hedge but decided it had been a fox or some other creature out for an evening stroll. She jumped when she heard a rustling sound and stood still, but there was nothing to see. She knew she was just feeling nervous because she still felt upset about Dan's odd behaviour.

When she got to the cottage, though, her gate was hanging open. She was certain she had closed it and felt a tremor of anxiety.

She looked around but could see nothing. Maybe the movement she had heard in the lane had been someone leaving.

She noticed the plant trough had been moved aside. Clearly, someone had been looking for the key that was now no longer there. Perhaps the camera had taken a picture. She opened the door and went inside. Everything looked as she had left it. Perhaps she hadn't shut the gate after all.

She looked at the camera and saw that a picture had been taken. She pressed the buttons as Dan had told her and saw a fuzzy shape looking through her letter box. There was no way in the world anyone could recognise the would-be intruder. He was wearing some sort of hood, so she couldn't actually tell if it was man or woman, child or adult.

She locked the door firmly behind her.

★ ★ ★

It was still early and Jess decided it was too soon to go to bed. She would never sleep, anyway, in her current state of mind. There was nothing she wanted to watch on television, so she poured herself a glass of wine and took it upstairs to Auntie May's old room. She dragged out one of the precious boxes and began to look through endless piles of old receipts, letters and guarantees for things long since cast out.

It was all rather fascinating. It gave a clear picture of the way May had lived over the past years.

Jess lifted out a pile of envelopes and flicked through them quickly. There seemed little of interest and she pushed everything back into the box.

There were two more boxes, one large and one smaller, that hadn't yet been explored.

She opened the smaller box. More letters. Some were tied together with a ribbon. She picked up one envelope and looked at writing that seemed familiar. Surely it was her father's hand? She opened the envelope and looked at the date. Nineteen-seventy-eight . . . three years before she was born.

'Dear May,' she read. 'You will be sorry to hear that Sarah has been unwell and has lost the baby she was carrying. We are both devastated and little Kim is very sad, too. She was so looking forward to having a baby brother or sister. Sadly, it also means that Sarah might not be able to have another child, and after my own illness, the doctors do not give us much hope of future success. We don't know what to do, as it is all too recent and painful. The possibilities are somewhat limited. We never wanted to have an only child. I always felt I'd missed out so much on a large family, being an only one myself. We hope to come down in a few weeks to get some sea air and give Kim a bit of a holiday. Hope that's all right with you? I'll write again soon. Love from us all, Bill.'

Jess stared at the words for a long time. She never knew that her mother had lost a baby before she was born. Did Kim remember? She had never mentioned it if she did. At two years old, she must have been too small to realise what was going on. At least the prognosis of no more babies had been wrong. She was the living proof. Wasn't she?

She stared at the letter in her hand. Unless . . . did this mean . . . could this mean that she, Jess, was adopted? Surely her parents would have told her if she was? No, it was not possible. She actually looked like her father. She didn't look much like Kim, but then her sister favoured her mother's side of the family.

Suddenly there was a loud banging at her door and Jess jumped out of her skin. Who on earth could be calling at this time of night? She left the precious box on the bed and went down the stairs.

'Who is it?' she called out.

'It's me, Dan. Sorry if I disturbed you.'

She opened the door.

He said, 'You weren't asleep were you?'

'No. I was just sorting through some stuff of my aunt's.'

'I'm glad to see you don't open the

door without asking who's there. Good girl.'

'Come in. Can I offer you something? Tea? Wine?' She felt anxious. What was he doing here after his earlier brush-off?

'A glass of wine would be great. Look, I'm sorry about my bad temper before. Can we talk?'

'Yes, please. I'd like that.'

A Devastating Discovery

'I was pretty mad when I called out to you and you turned away and ran off. I couldn't think what I might have done to annoy you,' Dan began.

'As I said, I wasn't even in town the day you claimed to have seen me. Perhaps I've got a double,' Jess said.

'If that's true, it was quite uncanny, and in that case, my apologies. I felt hurt at what I saw as a rejection from you.'

Jess felt her heart give a lurch. It seemed that Dan really did care.

'I just want you to know,' she told him, 'that I have every intention of coming back here. Permanently. I want to make this my home. I really love it here. Well, apart from my visitor. I did get a picture on your camera, by the way.'

'Any use?'

'Not really. I can't even tell if it's a male or female. I just find it all very strange and, well, a bit worrying, I suppose.' Jess paused. Suppose she really did have cousins living near? It was possible. And there could be a family likeness. Oh, it was all too much. Too complicated.

'You've gone very quiet suddenly. Something wrong?' Dan said.

'Not really. Just some family stuff I've been looking at. At least you're the image of your father, so you can't have any doubts,' she added.

'Now I am intrigued. You mean you don't look like your father?'

Jess looked away. It was too soon to voice any of her thoughts.

'You ready for another glass of wine?'

'She says, skilfully changing the subject. Anyway, I'm delighted you plan to come down here to live permanently.'

They talked about future possibilities and it was quite obvious that Dan was thinking of their relationship in the long term. It was exciting, if not slightly scary, considering they'd met only recently. They knew so little of each other but then, in all honesty, he wasn't the sole reason for Jess's decision. It was May's cottage that had clinched it for her. Dan was the icing on the cake.

'So, do you think the person I saw could be a relation of yours?' Dan asked.

'I'm just not sure. We know there were relations around here somewhere.'

'It strikes me as being odd that whoever it was ran away.'

'Maybe she didn't like being accosted in the street by a suspicious looking chap like you.' They both laughed and Dan got up from his chair.

'On that note, I'd better leave you. I'm so sleepy I'll never be up for milking in the morning.'

'I don't know how you cope. I'd never manage to get up at five every day.'

'You get used to it. And Dad does give me a day off every now and again.'

★　★　★

The house felt empty after Dan left and Jess felt restless. Since reading the letter from her father to May, she had felt oddly betrayed. She couldn't believe she was adopted but it clearly said that her parents had had problems of some sort. Perhaps if Kim was their only true child, that would explain why she had so often felt her sister was a favourite. There was nothing tangible, but she had always felt that Kim had done everything right in her parents' eyes. She'd married a man they approved of and presented them with the perfect pair of grandchildren. Though they always seemed proud of Jess being a teacher, it wasn't the same as being married and producing babies for them to coo over.

She went back into May's old room and looked again at the papers spread over the bed.

She read her father's letter again. What illness had he suffered? She knew nothing of his being unwell. In fact, he was always in remarkably good health.

She began to jot down some details.

What did she have so far? Her aunt (now, possibly, not a true relative at all) had a sister, June. They fell out when June married Mary's fiancé, Derek. June and Derek had two children. Derek had died in nineteen-ninety-one. The newspaper had said he left a son and daughter, April and Julian, and two grandchildren, David and Poppy. Maybe she could find out something about them. Old newspaper records. Parish records. Electoral rolls. All sorts of things were available. Tracing family history was quite easy these days.

She decided not to say anything to her parents at this stage. She would make her searches and then speak to them when she got home.

She continued her list. Julian would definitely be called Wishart. If she had married, April would have a different name. She went downstairs to find the telephone directory. She looked through the names and found several people named Wishart living in the area. She could phone some of them the next day and see . . . see what? She didn't really know what she could possibly say to them.

After breakfast next morning, she decided that a day spent finishing her search through old letters and papers seemed like a good plan.

There weren't all that many more to go and the answers she was looking for might be there.

She began reading again. Bills and receipts: lists: records of the dogs May had and their various vaccinations. Did she always keep everything? Jess pushed it all back into the box and felt slightly disappointed.

She looked in the wardrobe. There was another small box tucked away at the back. She pulled it out and sat on the bed to open it. More letters. She saw a much-thumbed envelope and slid out a letter. It was from Derek. She felt tears burn as she started to read the words. They were much too personal. May would have hated anyone else to read those words of love, meant for her eyes only. She put it to one side, intending to burn it when she could. Those words must remain between May and the lost love of her life.

Intriguingly, the letter had been written only days before Derek had married June.

There were a couple more letters in her father's writing. Both were thank you letters following a stay at the cottage and told her nothing new. Jess gave a sigh as she realised she had reached the final little bundle of letters. One of these was also in her father's writing, dated nineteen-eighty, the year before her own birth. Her fingers trembled as she took out the sheets of paper.

Dear May,

You'll be delighted for us when you know that at last Sarah is expecting a child. It's been a difficult time for us and some tough decisions had to be made. As you know, we had discovered that I was no longer able to father a child myself, but then modern science came to our aid. I may not be the actual biological father of this baby, but in every way, I am and always will be, his or her real parent. It was a difficult decision for us both but we have so much more love to give and we have always longed for another cherished child to make our family complete.

Our new addition is due in five months. Sarah is feeling fine and little Kim is over the moon at the prospect of a brother or sister. She's already planning games for them to share and has even offered her beloved teddy for the new baby.

We hope to come down to visit next summer, so you will meet the newest family member then. Naturally, we are not telling anyone else about this particular train of events but I needed to share it with someone and you are the nearest thing to a mother in my life.

With fondest love, Geoff.

★ ★ ★

Jess sat stock still. She felt slightly sick. This was devastating news. Kim was only her half sister and her father had nothing at all to do with her. Who on earth was her biological father? Did it really matter? In her father's own words, *I am and always will be his or her real parent*. All the same, it was a shock. She wondered if Kim knew and why she herself had never been told. Would it really have made any difference if she had known?

She went downstairs and grabbed her mobile phone, intent on calling her parents immediately, to try to discover the truth. Then she paused. Maybe she needed to get her head round all this before she jumped in with both feet. Besides, they were still staying with Kim, her sister. Her half sister. It would be better to wait until they were back in their own home. It might even be better to wait until she could tackle the problem face to face.

Jess decided she should call the police again the next morning. Oddly enough, she was disturbed more than frightened. The visitor looked small in stature and physically no match for her.

'It's a female,' she thought. She stood staring out of the window, deep in thought. It must be someone who lived nearby. Someone who could see exactly what her movements were. Someone who knew when she went out and when she arrived home.

She looked down the lane. There were very few houses. Apart from Dan and his family, she hadn't spoken to anyone else. Perhaps she would ask Dan if he knew who everyone was. She yawned. It had been a strange day. She had learned things she wished she hadn't, but she had also made some decisions and some plans.

* * *

Jess rose early, anxious to start the next phase of her family search. She was

She felt tears burning. Her whole world seemed to have collapsed. Everything she had held as familiar and secure now seemed unreal and somehow tainted. She felt very much alone.

She read and re-read the letter. Her mind was in a turmoil. She went for a long walk to try to clear her head.

She stood on the beach watching the waves on their endless journey back and forth along the shoreline of the little bay. May and her sister, June, had been children here and probably played in this very spot. She perched on a rock and tried to find some respite from her racing thoughts as she breathed in the clean air with its hint of salt and seaweed. She watched the gulls, immaculate in their grey and white livery, as they pecked along the shoreline. What a simple life theirs was.

For the rest of the day, Jess churned through the consequences of what she had learned. Would her parents realise that Aunt May had kept so many letters? Would they be prepared to answer some of the questions storming round her brain?

And did it really matter? Her parents were the same people she had known and loved all of her life. And trusted. But it was the trust that was shaken. They had lied to her by omission about the biggest thing in her life — her identity.

She finally decided to say nothing to her parents for the time being. Tomorrow, she would try to contact some of the people with entries under Wishart in the phone book. Hopefully, she could go and see anyone who might be related to the family.

She flicked on the television and gave a sudden jolt. She had forgotten to feed the cat and kittens. Some caring owner she was! She quickly put some food in a dish and went out into the twilight. The shed door was left open so the cat could come and go as it wanted and she called out as she walked up the path. There was an answering miaow and the little cat ran out and rubbed against her legs.

'I'm sorry, little one, I was too busy thinking about myself to feed you. There you go.?'

Jess grinned, chiding herself for talking to a cat. Maybe people did that, but she felt a little silly. And lonely. What would it really be like living here permanently? She'd soon make friends, she supposed, and if she had a job, there would be work colleagues. And Dan. Certainly, if Dan became a more permanent part of her life, she would be more than happy to stay here.

She stroked the cat and went back inside. She noticed a light flashing on the camera. She pressed the buttons and sure enough, there was a photograph of the same hooded figure she had seen before. There was nothing to identify who it could be, but the person had clearly been looking in through the window while she had been outside. She gave a shudder. How did the know she had gone to feed the c unless they were watching her ev move? That wasn't a nice thought at

about to start phoning when the plumber arrived at her door.

'Got summat wrong with your drains, have you?' he said, as he walked inside her cottage. 'Tranter's the name. Is that coffee I can smell?'

She gave a grin. 'I can make some more if you'd like a cup.'

'Very civil of you. Rather have tea, though, if it's all the same to you. Milk and two sugars.'

'Sure,' Jess said resignedly. It looked as if her phone calls would have to wait, but it was good to know she was getting some essential work done. She made a mug of tea and took it upstairs to the plumber.

'You got a blockage. Not a problem. Have her fixed in no time. Just need a new bit of pipe and then you should maybe get the septic tank emptied. Know where she is, do you?'

'Not really. Down the garden I expect.' Jess grimaced. She had no idea about such things. 'Do you know someone who could look at it?'

'I'll get my lad on to it. Don't you worry. Lovely cuppa. Ta very much.'

The plumber seemed to know what he was doing, so Jess left him to it. An hour later, he came downstairs.

'She's all fixed up right as rain. Shouldn't have any trouble now. I'll send my lad round to empty your tank.'

'So, you staying here now?' Mr Tranter added. 'Sorry to see the old lady go. Nice woman she was. Always welcoming with tea and biscuits.'

'I'm planning to move down sometime soon,' Jess said.

'And what sort of job would you be looking out for?' Mr Tranter asked.

'I'm a teacher.'

'Oh dear. Oh dear me. Poor thing. Must be a terrible job.'

'I quite enjoy it actually,' Jess said with a laugh.

'Wouldn't do for me. Oh no, not at all. Plumbing doesn't answer back. Well, not much anyway.'

'Well, thank you very much Mr Tranter. What do I owe you?'

'I'll send you a bill. My wife handles all that stuff.'

'Okay. I'll look out for it.'

Jess then realised that, in Mr Tranter, she had the ideal person to tell her more about her neighbours.

'Do you know the other people who live along the lane?' she said casually. 'I haven't got round to meeting them yet.'

'Mostly they're holiday places. One or two get winter lets. Emmets, the lot of them.'

'You don't sound as if you approve.'

'Takes up all the homes local youngsters might have bought. Rich folks from up-country can afford silly prices while our children have to leave the county.'

'I hadn't thought of it like that.'

'Terrible it is. Well I'd best get on now. Be seeing you.'

★ ★ ★

Jess watched the plumber drive off and went back inside, ready to start making her phone calls. She felt slightly apprehensive, wondering what sort of reception she might get.

She had a list of seven numbers to call. The first three didn't answer. The next was some sort of souvenir shop. They didn't know anything about her aunt's sister.

The next one was a better prospect. It seemed that new people had bought what had been June's old house. They were able to tell Jess that June was now in a nursing home just outside Penzance. It seemed she was not in good health.

Jess looked up the number of the nursing home and dialled it. She was trembling slightly at the thought of possibly speaking to the woman about whom she had discovered some things, not all of them pleasant.

She spoke to the owner of the nursing home and arranged to visit later that afternoon. She said she was a relative of June's.

'Mrs Wishart likes a bit of a rest after

her lunch. About three-thirty might be best,' she was told.

'Thank you. I'll be there. Is there anything she might like that I could bring for her?'

'She's always partial to a few chocolates. But don't bring a big box. She'll eat the lot in one go and make herself ill. And I should warn you, she does get a little confused at times.'

'Okay, thanks.'

Jess was trembling slightly when she put down the phone. She felt oddly emotional. A week ago, she hadn't even known about June Wishart.

She gave a start as the phone rang. It was Dan.

'Sorry I haven't been in touch. I was really busy yesterday. So, what have you been up to?'

Jess told him about her planned visit that afternoon.

'Oh, that's a pity. I was going to ask if you'd like to come out for a sail with me.'

'Oh Dan, I'd have loved to. But I'm

committed now. I'm going to see my aunt's sister. The one I told you about. She married May's fiancé just before they were due to get married. But as for sailing, maybe another day?'

'Course. It was short notice, anyhow. Thought it was worth asking. Maybe you'd like a drink this evening? Then you can tell me all about this mysterious new aunt of yours.'

'She's not exactly my aunt, more second cousin nine times removed or something.'

'I'll pick you up around seven. We can have a bite to eat, and you can explain your entire complicated family tree.'

★ ★ ★

Jess spent the next hour trying to decide what to wear. Her wardrobe was very limited as most of her things were still back at home. She wanted to look nice. Smart, but not off-putting. She also needed to stop somewhere to buy some chocolates. But what sort? Milk or plain? Soft or hard centres? She stopped and breathed deeply. She. was being stupid. Why get so worked up about a simple visit to an elderly lady? But it wasn't just a simple visit, was it? It was far more than that.

It was a chance to find out the truth about her family and, perhaps, her very existence.

Dan Talks Of Love

The Hollies was an old country house which had been converted to make an imposing nursing home. Jess parked in the wide drive and rang the bell. A woman in uniform answered and led her into the large sitting room. Several ladies were dozing in their armchairs and a television was playing in one corner.

Jess was led to an old lady who looked like her Aunt May, or what Jess could remember of her.

'Hello Aunt June,' she said softly. 'I'm Jess Cunningham. Bill's daughter.'

The old lady looked at Jess with a frown.

'I don't remember asking you to come for tea.'

'You didn't. I'm staying here for a

while and thought it would be nice for us to meet. I've brought you some chocolates.'

'You're not Poppy, are you? I have a granddaughter called Poppy. She looks like you but younger.'

'I believe she does look like me,' Jess said, remembering Dan's encounter with someone he'd thought was her.

'Are you the one May left her cottage to?' June asked with a sudden clarity.

'Yes, that's right.'

Jess noticed a change coming over the old lady. She had become tense and agitated.

'You've stolen my family's birthright,' she accused. 'That sister of mine had no right leaving the cottage outside the family. We were brought up there. It was our home. My parents had no right leaving it to her. It was never easy, you know, bringing up two children in a rented house.' After this outburst, the old lady was silent.

Jess bit her lip. She should have realised there would be some anger at what June must have considered to be the loss of the family home. But, sister or no sister, why would May have left her property to someone who had wronged her so?

Jess took the plunge. 'I expect May thought the family connection was done when you and Derek were married.'

June glared at her visitor.

'Derek loved me. He never wanted that old frump. He wanted me. I was pretty and always looked nice. I gave him babies. Two lovely babies we had.'

'He died you know, my Derek. I miss him.' The old lady looked tearful and Jess felt guilty that she'd stirred long-ago memories.

'I know. I'm sorry,' she said. Then added, 'So, do your family still live in the area? Do they come and see you?'

'They do. Well, some of them do. But they're always so busy. Poppy, my granddaughter, lives somewhere outside Cornwall but she comes to see me when she can. I don't know what happened to April, her mother. She was such a pretty little girl. But she's gone away now. Strange little thing she was. I don't see her at all now. My Julian still comes, though. Every week or so.'

'I want my tea now. And I don't think I want to see you again. You stole my family's home. Go away.'

Jess sighed. 'Goodbye, then. I'll leave my phone number with the nurses and if you do want me to visit again, they can ring and let me know.'

'I shan't want to see *you* again. Ever.'

'Very well. I'm sorry, I'd have liked to talk some more, but if you want me to leave, I will.'

Jess stood up, but June did not acknowledge her.

Before leaving, Jess went to see the matron of the Home.

'I wondered if I could leave my contact number with you?' she said. 'My . . . my aunt seemed unwilling to see me again but just in case she changes her mind . . .'

'Don't worry about it,' the matron

said. 'She has her off days and might well want to see you again.'

Jess hesitated, then thought she might as well go for it. 'I suppose you couldn't give me her son, Julian's, address, could you?'

'I could pass your details on to him. But I couldn't divulge his information.'

'I quite understand. Thank you. I'd be grateful if you would pass on my details. I'm hoping to meet them before I leave Cornwall.'

'I'll certainly give him your address. And thank you for visiting. June doesn't get many visitors. Julian comes occasionally, but not often. She doesn't always welcome him.'

Jess passed over her contact details and left. Things may not have gone quite as she had hoped, but she felt optimistic about the possibility of meeting the rest of the family at some point.

The thought of the evening ahead with Dan cheered her, too, and she drove home in a lighter mood. Home.

She realised she had thought of the cottage as home.

* * *

Once Jess got inside the cottage, she checked the camera to see if there had been any callers while she had been out. With a shiver of fear, she saw that the same hooded figure had been to the door and then peered in through the windows. She remembered her cat and kittens and went out to look for them. The makeshift bed was empty and there was no sign of the little family. She called them, but they didn't appear. She felt bad as she thought of her neglect the previous day, when she had forgotten to feed them. She put out some food for them anyway, and went back inside the cottage. She made some tea and sat with her hands wrapped round the mug. Her thoughts went to Dan. He and his family seemed so uncomplicated and happy together.

She had thought her own family had

been the same. But now everything had changed. She wondered exactly how much she should tell Dan of her discoveries.

★ ★ ★

'So, where are we going this evening?' Jess said, when Dan arrived to pick her up.

'Little pub along the coast. They have a curry night tonight. You do like curry, don't you?'

'Yes, I do. Occasionally, that is. It makes a nice change. Did you go sailing?' she asked.

'No. Thought maybe we'd go another day. I keep a dinghy down at the beach.'

'I've never actually been sailing out on the sea,' Jess said. 'I sailed on a lake with a school trip once, though.'

'It's very different on the sea. There are the winds for one thing. They make such a difference to the amount of tacking you have to do.' Dan talked with enthusiasm about his boat and

116

sailing until they drew up in the car park of the pub. 'Sorry,' he said, 'once I get started, its difficult to stop me! How did you get on today?'

Jess sighed. 'Not very well. My aunt believes I stole her birthright by being left the cottage. And she doesn't want to see me again. Bit sad, really, but I suppose I can understand.'

'Maybe so. May did get the cottage but June had the man and the family.'

Jess nodded. 'I suppose that's one way to look at it. Oh, by the way, I think it may have been my distant cousin you saw in town the other day. Evidently she looks like me. Amazing, really, when you consider I'm not actually related.'

'What do you mean?' Dan said.

Jess closed her eyes. She hadn't meant to say anything to Dan, but it was so much on her mind that her comment had just slipped out. She told him what she had discovered about her parentage.

'So you see, it seems that my dad

isn't really my biological father at all. I haven't spoken to my parents yet. It's all a bit new and takes some getting used to.'

'What a thing to discover, just like that. You're absolutely sure? I mean, couldn't you have misunderstood the letter?'

'No. I'm quite sure.'

'But surely your dad is the one who brought you up? Played games with you. Gave you a hug when you needed it. Handed out pocket money. Loved you.'

'Yes, I know. I do know. I shouldn't have said anything to you.'

'I'm glad you did.' He reached over and took her hand, stroking her fingers gently as he spoke. 'I want to find out everything about you.'

'That's scary,' she replied with a grin.

The conversation returned to a lighter vein and the evening passed quickly. Jess told Dan about the plumber's visit and how she had enjoyed listening to his Cornish accent.

Dan proved he was locally born and bred by chatting in the same accent. She giggled. 'You do it perfectly. Most people trying to imitate it sound really bad.'

'Well, I was born here and went to school here.'

'But you don't speak like that most of the time. Nor do your parents.'

'You should hear them when they're angry! The accent pours out in spades.'

'I can't imagine your mum ever getting really cross.'

'We know better than to give her cause,' Dan laughed.

At the end of the evening, he saw her in and checked the camera for unexpected visitors. There were none.

'I've decided my mysterious caller must be a woman,' Jess said. 'I also think it must be someone who lives close. She seems to know when I go out, so she might be able to see this place from where she lives. I was going to ask you who lives down this lane?'

'They're all holiday lets, I think.'

'That's pretty much what the plumber said.'

'There's one apartment in that larger house at the top, where the caretaker lives,' Dan said. 'I'm afraid that's about all I know. Look, you are all right, aren't you?'

'Yes, I suppose so. Strangely enough, I don't feel threatened. I'd like to meet whoever it is and find out why she's hanging around so much. What does she want?'

'Just be careful, Jess. I don't want you taking any risks.'

'I won't. But thank you for your concern. It's nice to know you care.'

'I'd like to care a lot, Jess,' Dan said, stroking her hair gently. 'But I don't want to fall in love with you and then you go back to somewhere miles away. I'm really tied to Cornwall and farming.'

'Don't worry. I have every intention of coming back to live here when I sort out my job situation. I have to work my notice, probably till Christmas, but I can always come down at weekends and certainly for half term.'

He took her into his arms.

'Maybe I can allow myself to fall in love with you in that case,' he said softly, before kissing her.

'I'd better go now,' he said. 'Early start and all that. Sleep well and remember, your family will always be your family, whatever happens.'

'I know, goodnight, Dan. And thanks for listening.'

She shut the door behind him and locked it. She leaned against it, smiling to herself. He said he might fall in love with her. She hugged herself in delight.

★ ★ ★

Jess slept well and woke refreshed. The sun was shining and she went into the garden to eat her breakfast. There was so much that needed to be done out here, she thought. Perhaps her parents might come down and help her. That way, she could show them Auntie May's letter, and they could explain everything to her. She decided she would invite them down as soon as they came back from their stay with Kim. Meanwhile, there were still a couple of phone numbers she could call. Two more people named Wishart. After meeting June, though, she felt apprehensive about the reception she might receive from other members of the family. Perhaps it would be best to wait a couple more days to see if Julian might call.

There were still plenty of chores to occupy her and she decided to plan her arrangements for the upstairs of the cottage. Would she keep the little room she had used when she had stayed here as a child? Or should she take over Auntie May's old room? Or the guest room? She stood in each room for a few minutes, looking out of the windows and trying to decide which had the best view. Undoubtedly, it was Auntie May's room. There were glimpses of the sea from there. But she wasn't entirely comfortable with the idea. Maybe if she were to redecorate the room it would seem better. More hers.

On impulse, she decided to go out to buy paint. She had some savings to spare. It would be good to spend them on making the cottage truly hers. It might be nice to get some new curtains, too, and some matching bedding. She hunted round the house to find a measuring tape for the curtains, but she couldn't find one. She used a piece of string to measure the length instead. It would have to do.

As she passed the phone, she hesitated. Should she make a call before she went out or wait to see if Julian called her? She decided to wait. She didn't want to face another rejection.

She drove to Penzance and parked outside a large D.I.Y store. She got a trolley and found the paint department. She decided on plain white, as the rooms had only small windows and were prone to be rather dark. She could add colour with cushions and curtains.

She collected packs of assorted brushes and a roller set and made for the soft furnishing department, where she enjoyed herself choosing cushions, sheets, duvet covers and matching curtains. She chose pretty floral patterns in keeping with the cottage atmosphere. With her trolley loaded to the brim, she went to the check-out.

'Poppy, dear, is it really you?' Someone touched her shoulder and she turned to face a woman who was quite unfamiliar to her. 'Oh, I'm so sorry,' the woman said. 'I mistook you for someone else. You must have a double, dear.'

'I've been told I have,' Jess replied, remembering Dan's incident with the girl who looked like her.

'I wonder if you're related?' the woman asked. 'Sorry, I'm an old friend of the family. You look uncannily like Poppy.'

Jess took a gamble.

'Would that be Poppy Wishart, by any chance?'

'Well, yes. Are you related?'

'I might be. Do you know if the family still live locally?'

The woman looked uncomfortable and a lot less friendly. Jess ploughed on.

'I went to see my Aunt June yesterday but she wasn't really very pleased to see me.'

'Then you must be the girl who got May's house. Caused a lot of bad feeling, that did.'

'I'm sure. But I'd really like to get in contact with the family. Perhaps you could mention that you met me?'

'I'll mention it. Excuse me now. I must get on.'

'Wait. Can I give you my phone number? Just in case they want to talk to me?'

'I suppose so. But I've no idea when I shall see them again.'

Jess scribbled her number on a piece of paper and handed it to the woman.

'Thank you very much. It was nice meeting you.'

The woman nodded and walked away quickly.

Jess wondered if she would ever hear from Julian and his family. Clearly she was regarded by all as a usurper and an unwelcome intruder. She sighed and went to pay for her purchases.

A Surprising Phone Call

The camera light was flashing when Jess got back to the cottage. She pressed the button and saw the now familiar hooded figure peering in at the window. But this time there was a second picture. It was clearly Dan, who was smiling up at her. She was sorry to have missed him. She dialled his number.

'I was just passing,' he told her. 'I came to see if there was any coffee going. You been somewhere nice?'

'I decided to re-decorate so I've spent a fortune at the DIY store.'

'Do you need a hand? I've got a couple of hours to spare this afternoon. And I'd enjoy spending time with you.'

It was soon arranged. Dan would come round after lunch and they would make a start. There was a lot to do before the actual painting could begin and it would be helpful to have someone to help move the heavy old furniture.

Jess realised she was feeling hungry. She grilled some cheese on toast, then remembered a plum tree in the garden and went out to see if there were any ripe ones yet.

To her delight, the cat came to greet her so she went back to fetch some food for her. The kittens were romping around the overgrown lawn, hiding among the bushes and pouncing on imaginary prey. They were delightful little things. She wanted to keep one or two of them if she possibly could. She frowned. What a pity it was that she had to return and work out another term at school. But there was nothing else she could do. Teaching had contracts and there was no alternative.

The plums were very sour and one was enough to convince her they needed longer on the tree. She heard Dan's car stop and went to greet him.

★ ★ ★

They worked steadily, piling stuff on the spare bed. There were so many ornaments and bits and pieces, Jess began to despair.

'What on earth shall I do with all these?' she said. 'I hate to throw them out but I can't live with all this.'

'There are plenty of antique shops. Some of these might be worth money if you really don't want them.'

'It seems awful to sell off Auntie May's treasures. Maybe I should just store them somewhere. Perhaps her family might like them as keepsakes.'

'From what you've told me, I doubt that. They don't sound like major fans.' Jess had already told Dan about her encounter in the DIY store and about being mistaken for Poppy.

★ ★ ★

Dan was clearly experienced at decorating and he took charge of the proceedings. Jess followed his instructions and vacuumed walls, ceiling and floor while he washed down the woodwork.

'Are we painting the woodwork?' he asked.

'Do you think I should?'

'It might look a bit grubby with everything else looking pristine white.'

He reached over and touched her arm. 'You know, it gives me great encouragement to see you doing this. Decorating, I mean. It gives me confidence that you definitely are moving in.'

'It could also mean that I'm planning to do the place up to sell it, or even let it out,' Jess grinned.

Dan laughed. 'I don't think you'd be quite so enthusiastic about all the things you've bought if that were the case.'

Jess smiled at him. 'You're right, of course. And I'm getting more enthusiastic by the minute. I was only thinking today that I wish I could just stay here now. But I have to go back and teach for another term. No way out of it.'

'I've blown a load of my savings today and I need to spend heaps more. There's so much I want to do. New chairs and sofa in the lounge. Lots of things in the kitchen.'

Dan sighed. 'I'm going to miss you. You'd be away from September to Christmas.'

'Like I said, I shall come down for weekends. And there's half term. It'll soon pass.'

Dan took her in his arms. 'Maybe we've only just met,' he said, 'but you've become part of my life.'

Jess felt her heart beat a lot faster. She knew it would take very little for her to admit that she had fallen in love with Dan.

He kissed her and then let her go. 'You really should stop distracting me. I can stay for another half hour and then I must go and see to the cows. Oh, by the way, Mum said to bring you back for supper.'

'That's really kind of her, but I couldn't impose.'

'I said you'd say that, but she says, as she's cooking for us anyway, one extra portion is nothing. Say yes or she'll tell me off. She'll say I didn't invite you properly.'

'You sound really scared of your Mum,' Jess laughed.

'Oh I am. Truly. So, you'll come then?'

'Well, thank you. I'll come round in a little while when you've had time to do the milking.'

'OK. I'd better go and get started. See you in a little while.'

He went downstairs and she heard him slam the door. She smiled and hugged herself. She felt very happy.

She glanced at her watch. She ought to call her parents and invite them down, but decided against it. Better to wait until she had finished the decorating and then they could see the results of her efforts.

She heard her mobile ringing and ran

down to answer it.

'Is that Miss Cunningham? Jessica?' asked a male voice.

'Speaking.'

'I understand you've been looking for me. I am Julian Wishart.'

Jess's heart leapt. She couldn't believe he had actually called.

'Julian,' she said. 'thank you so much for calling. I was hoping we might meet?'

'I'm not sure about that. This is merely a courtesy call. I can't think we have anything to say to each other. My neighbour passed on your message and I don't want her to be bothered again. I'm sure you know that my family and May had very little to do with each other. In fact, my mother always becomes very distressed when her sister is mentioned.'

'Did you know I went to see her yesterday? In the nursing home?'

'Oh, dear me. No, I didn't know. I hope you didn't upset her.'

'Not intentionally. But she did seem rather angry. She told me I'd stolen her birthright.'

'That's probably the way we all feel, if I'm honest.'

'Well, I'm sorry you feel that way.'

'How could we feel anything else? You're a distant member of the family and somehow you've managed to find yourself living in what should have been my family's home.'

'I'm sorry,' Jess said. 'I'd hoped we might be able to meet and at least talk civilly.'

'I'll give it some thought.'

'Thank you. And thank you for phoning me. I really do hope to hear from you again.'

Julian hung up and Jess switched off her mobile. She stared at it thoughtfully. She had been naïve in thinking the family would welcome her. The resentments obviously ran deep and Julian probably had no inkling that his mother had gone off with May's fiancé. Possibly June had told him a different story altogether and he never knew that May was the injured party.

* ★ *

Jess tidied up her decorating materials, had a shower and changed. It wasn't too early to go round to Dan's, so she locked up carefully and set off down the lane. It was a pleasant evening and she felt content. At the farm, she stood leaning over the gate, watching as Dan herded the cows back to the pasture. They ambled slowly along, knowing their route and exactly what was expected of them. She smiled and raised a hand as Dan saw her. He came across.

'I knew you couldn't resist seeing my beauties.'

'I was just thinking how calm and placid they are. Not a care in the world.'

'They're well looked after and used to their routine. I reckon they could come in and attach themselves to the milking machines!'

'Come on, let's go inside. I'll go and clean up and you can chat to Mum.

She's delighted I've found a friend so close to home. A special friend.'

Jess felt her cheeks reddening as her heart raced.

Dan touched her arm as he opened the door, gesturing her inside the warm kitchen.

'Hello dear,' Mrs Meadows said cheerfully. 'It's rather hot in here. Prop the door open, Dan, before I faint.'

'Are you sure you don't mind me descending on you again?' Jess said.

She was reassured and the friendly little woman busied herself with the pots on the cooker as she chatted nineteen to the dozen. There were some delicious aromas filling the kitchen and Jess felt her stomach rumbling in anticipation.

'I hope you're hungry,' Mrs Meadows said, as if reading her mind. 'Dan said you've been working hard.'

'I'm starving,' Jess laughed. 'And you're such a good cook. I could never hope to match you.'

'Nonsense, dear. It's a matter of

decent ingredients and a bit of know-how. You'll soon learn. I dare say you had your nose in a book most of the time and your mum probably did all the cooking.'

'You're quite right. My limit seems to be things on toast.'

'Well, now, there's a start. Now where's our Dan to?'

'Where's he to? What do you mean?'

'Cornish. Means where is he? There's a whole lot of lovely old Cornish sayings. You'll soon pick up on them when you've been around for a while. You are planning to stay round, I hope?'

Jess was spared repeating her needs to return up-country as they all called it, as Dan and his father came in.

A huge meat pie was placed on the table, along with heaped dishes of fresh butttered vegetables. Stewed plums and custard followed and everyone sat back to relax.

'That was another magnificent meal,' Jess said. 'Thank you so much.' She looked across the table at Dan. 'I had a call from my distant cousin, Julian, after you left,' she told him. 'None too friendly, but at least he made contact.'

'I reckon he must be well into his fifties. His daughter may be a bit older than me, but evidently looks very like me. We've been mistaken for each other a couple of times,' she told Mrs Meadows, grinning at Dan.

'Absolute double,' Dan agreed.

'Genes will out, they do say,' Mrs Meadows said.

Jess looked uncomfortable but said nothing. Dan changed the subject by inviting her to have another walk round the farm.

'I'll come along with you,' Dan's father said. 'I want to take a look at the big field. Might be ready to cut the second crop of hay.'

'Leave them to go on their own,' Mrs Meadows chided. 'For goodness sake, you can walk over to that field any old time.' Mr Meadows glared at his wife but knew it was pointless to argue with her. Dan and Jess made their escape.

'So, tell me about this man, Julian,' Dan said.

'He wasn't particularly friendly,' Jess told him. 'His neighbour had passed on my message and he claimed he didn't want her to be bothered again. I don't think he knows about May and his father. What on earth do you think caused Derek to marry June instead of May? She must have had some hold over him. He wrote to May just days from the wedding saying how much he loved her. And there's also a silver bangle with an eternal love message engraved inside.'

'How intriguing,' Dan said. 'But Julian's parents seemed to have had some sort of reasonable marriage. They had children, didn't they?'

'Yes, of course. Oh well, I don't suppose we shall ever know, not unless June can tell us anything.'

★ ★ ★

They walked hand in hand round the fields. Cows grazed placidly and hedges gave way to glimpses of the sea. 'This is such a beautiful place,' Jess murmured.

'Made even more beautiful by having you here with me. I can't bear the thought of you going away again,' Dan said.

'Nor me. But there's nothing I can do about it. I'll come down as often as I can.'

The peace was shattered when Jess's mobile phone rang. She gave a jump. 'I'm sorry. I forgot it was in my pocket.' She looked at the screen. 'It's my parents. Do you mind if I take the call?'

'Course not,' Dan said.

'Hello? Mum? Is everything all right?'

'Of course it is. I was just phoning to see how things are going. And to see if you'd like us to come down for a few days. Your father and I would love to see the old place again, and you did mention some gardening?'

'Well, yes, that would be great. But

I'm in the middle of decorating the main bedroom. When were you thinking of coming?'

'Next week, if possible. It's not all that long till term starts, is it, dear? If we don't make the effort soon, it will be too late.'

They agreed her parents would drive down on Monday morning.

'So I shall be seeing even less of you over the next week,' Dan said.

'Not necessarily. You might like to meet them. Unless you think it might be a bit too soon for that?'

'And exactly how long was it before you met my parents?'

'Okay. Fine. But you may get something of a third degree.'

'Not the, are your intentions honourable speech?' Dan said with a broad grin. 'I could have fun with that.'

'Behave,' she laughed, giving him a friendly punch on the arm.

He pulled her towards him and kissed her. She smiled up at him. 'I think we should maybe get back or your parents will be sending out a search party.'

They wandered slowly back to the pretty farmhouse as the sun was sinking, casting a deep reddish glow over the clouds.

'Red sky at night,' Dan said. 'Should be a nice day tomorrow. Maybe we could go for that sail?'

'Thanks, but I really need to get the decorating finished, especially now my parents are coming down.'

'Okay then, I'll come and help after I finish work. I'll bring some pasties round and we can have a late lunch.'

'You're too good to me.'

'I'm hoping so. I want to build up a huge debt of gratitude so you'll feel obliged to come and see me.'

★ ★ ★

Jess had a restless night. Now her parents were actually going to be here, she would have to tackle the questions that had filled her mind since she had looked through May's old letters. She wasn't ready for it, but she knew it had to be faced some time. She still hadn't made up her mind what she wanted to say. She wanted the truth confirmed but she didn't want to upset either of her parents. She wondered if they might know anything of the mystery as to why Derek married June and not May. It was going to be a strange visit, with so many issues to consider. It would also feel rather odd having them visit what was now her new home. Especially as it was a place they had known most of their married lives.

The next few days were spent in a flurry of activity. Dan came to help as much as he could and they shared several scratch meals, suppers at the pub and a magnificent Sunday roast at Dan's parents.

'Now, you must bring your parents round for supper one evening,' Mrs Meadows insisted as she cleared the plates. 'It will be lovely to see them again and catch up a bit.'

'Perhaps we could take you out for a meal,' Jess suggested. 'You've fed me for weeks now.'

'Dad doesn't like to eat out,' Dan said. 'He reckons they can't cook properly anywhere else.'

'I can understand that. If I could cook like you, Mrs Meadows, I guess I wouldn't want to eat out much either.'

'Why not bring your parents round tomorrow evening? They'll have had a long journey and won't feel like cooking.'

'You're very kind, but we'll be pleased to come a bit later in the week, if that's all right. We have quite a lot of talking to do.'

'Just as you please. Let our Dan know when it's convenient.'

Once coffee was over, Jess and Dan excused themselves. The decorating was finished and they had to move the furniture back into the bedroom. Jess was looking forward to seeing the final effect.

They walked back to the cottage and

let themselves in. Once more the light on the security camera was flashing, indicating that someone had visited. Dan looked at the picture. It was the same hooded figure.

'You're right,' Dan said, 'I think it is a female. I suspect it's not a young person, either. It's very strange.'

'Maybe she'll give up when my parents are here. Other people around might scare her off. I do find it rather odd, though. What can she hope to gain by looking in the window? And why doesn't she just come and knock on the door when I'm home?'

'Maybe we'll never know. Now, let's get this room sorted before I have to go and do the milking.'

It didn't take long and once the new covers were on the bed, the curtains hung and everything put straight, Jess stood back and looked on approvingly. 'Thank you so much, Dan. It looks super. I'm now wondering if I should have replaced the carpet, though. What do you think?'

'Maybe in time. Don't try to do everything at once. You need to live with things for a while and then decide. Besides, you'll end up in a muddle with everything half finished. Your parents should be suitably impressed, I'm sure. Now, what about all the boxes of stuff you've left in the other room?'

'I think they should stay there. I'm not sure how much my parents will want to look at, and there are some things I am going to keep private. Auntie May would never have wanted anyone to read some of her letters. They were so very personal. I shall burn them eventually.'

'You should maybe hold on to them for a little while longer. You never know, the answers to your many questions may be there. Now, if you'll excuse me, I have a large collection of females awaiting my attention.'

'I guess your precious cows will always come before me.'

'Naturally,' Dan grinned. 'But you do come a close second.'

'Seriously, though, thank you for all your help. I'd have got nowhere without you.'

'We make a good team. Now, go and have a rest. You've been working very hard.'

'I need to do some shopping before my parents get here. Hopefully, I'll manage to get out early in the morning.'

'Bye then. I'll leave you with your parents tomorrow, but phone me the next day.' He gave her a kiss, and went off down the lane.

After he had gone, Jess wandered round the garden, trying to tell herself she was making plans for the gardening her father might attempt.

In reality, she was wondering how on earth she was going to bring up the subject of her parentage.

Jess Confronts Her Parents

Jess went out to feed the cat and kittens early next morning. The box was empty and she could see no sign of them. She left the dish of food and wondered if they had finally departed. Dan had suggested they might, as they were feral cats, used to fending for themselves around the farm buildings. She felt slightly disappointed as she'd hoped to keep at least one of them. But, as she had to leave when the new school term began, she supposed it was more sensible that they should have gone.

She glanced at her watch. She expected her parents around lunch-time, so she needed to get to the shops.

There were still plenty of holiday-makers around and the supermarket was busy for a Monday morning. Jess

148

stocked up on all the things she knew her parents liked. She doubted they would actually eat at home very much, though. Her father always enjoyed pub meals, especially when he was on holiday.

She smiled. It was a sort of holiday, she supposed, even though both parents would probably insist on cleaning and tidying up the garden and the house, just as they always did when staying at her sister's house. Half-sister, Jess realised with a jolt.

When she arrived back at the cottage, her parents had already arrived. Her father was looking around the garden and her mother was sitting on a bench in the sun.

'Goodness, you must have set out at the crack of dawn to get here so early,' Jess said. 'I'm sorry I wasn't here. I went to the supermarket to stock up.'

'Hello, darling,' her mother said, hugging her. 'You look tired. I hope you haven't been overdoing things.'

'Course not. I didn't sleep much last

night, that's all.'

'Hello, my darling,' her father called, as he walked up the garden. 'You're looking good. Fresh sea air and sunshine obviously agrees with you.'

'I thought she was looking tired,' her mother argued. Jess grinned; it was good to see them. 'I can't wait for you to come and see what I've done to the cottage. You'd be proud of me, Mum.'

'We always are, Jess,' replied her father. Her adoptive father. This was so difficult. He put his arm round her and she felt his comforting presence wash over her. He was her dad. Of course he was, and always would be.

'I'll just get the shopping, then we can go in and have some coffee,' she said.

They carried the bags inside and Jess began putting things away. 'Put the kettle on, Mum, and I'll be with you in a mo.'

'What's this contraption flashing away in the corner?'

'Oh, it's just the security thing Dan

set up. Nothing to worry about.'

'Dan? Who's Dan? And why do you need security? Jessica, what's been going on?' her mother demanded.

She told them the whole story of the coffee-making, the gardening and all the times the woman had peered through the window. She reassured them that the police had been told and that everything was fine.

'I knew there was something wrong. I just knew it,' her mother, Sarah, said anxiously. 'You're not safe here in the middle of nowhere and all alone.'

'Mum, I'm fine, really.'

'So, who is this Dan you mentioned?' her father asked.

'Dan Meadows. Son of the farmer next door. They've invited you round for supper one night. Mrs Meadows is one fabulous cook. She says she remembers you from way back.'

'Small woman. Bright little button eyes and rules her men with a rod of iron,' her father, Bill, said.

'Absolutely right. Add on the heart of

gold and you get the complete picture.'

'And tell us about this Dan. How old is he and what's he like?'

'He's gorgeous. Tall, good looking and a bit older than me.'

'Serious then, is it?' her mother probed.

'Might be, given time.' Jess's cheeks burned and she lowered her eyes.

'Leave the poor girl alone, Sarah. She's only been down here for five minutes. So, what do you think of your new home? Will you move down here?' her father asked.

'Of course I will. I never doubted it, really. But I have to find a job. Mind you, the landlord at the local pub has offered me one.'

'You'll never starve, love,' Bill said cheerfully. 'You're far too clever for that.'

'And if I keep going round to the Meadows' for meals, I'll soon be like the back of a bus!'

★ ★ ★

They finished their coffee and went on a tour of inspection. Her parents were very impressed with the newly-decorated bedroom and delighted that Jess had offered it to them for their stay.

'There's still masses to do, of course, but at least I've made a start,' Jess said.

'You've done well. For someone who knows nothing about decorating, it's a fine job,' Bill said.

'I'll admit to having some help from Dan.'

'So when do we get to meet your Dan?' her mother asked.

'Soon. And he's not exactly *my* Dan.'

'Hadn't we better unload the car?' Bill said. 'Only I seem to remember you, Sarah, putting no end of food into the boot. Something about Jess having nothing in to eat?'

Jess grinned. Her mum was always the same.

They went out to the car and staggered back in with boxes of food, several suitcases and a number of plastic bags.

'I've brought you a few bits and pieces you might need,' her mother said to Jess. 'Bedding and towels and such. And I had a bit of a baking session. There's a pie for supper tonight and a few cakes and things. I'll put them in the pantry, shall I?'

'Thanks, Mum.'

'Do you want some help with May's personal stuff?' her father asked. 'I know she was a bit of a hoarder and there's probably a lot of things you need to sort through.'

'I think I've done most of it,' Jess said quickly. 'Now, what do you want for lunch?'

They chatted about what needed doing as they ate cheese and pickles with fresh bread, sitting outside in the sunshine. Bill was keen to make suggestions about the garden.

'You need a garden with very low maintenance. You could have a nice heather bed and a few shrubs. Maybe just one small bed for cut flowers. And how do you feel about vegetables? Do you want to grow them, too?'

'I suspect I'd be useless at it. But your other suggestions sound great, Dad. Maybe we can get started on the area nearest the house?'

'Sounds like a plan, and someone's done a bit, I see. Was that in one of your mad bursts of enthusiasm?'

'That was my mysterious intruder. Strange for someone virtually breaking into the place to stop and do some gardening.'

'Perhaps it's some pensioner who no longer has his own garden. Misses doing a bit of work.'

'I think it's a woman. Did Auntie May have anyone who used to come and help her?'

'Sadly, I don't know. We rather neglected her latterly. I expect she needed some help, though.'

The afternoon passed quickly as they pottered around the garden, and then they all went for a walk along the beach. The *do you remembers* came thick and fast as they talked of the many holidays spent here. The subject of May's family came up naturally in the conversation, and Jess was able to ask if her parents knew why Derek Wishart had married June and not May, his original fiancée.

'It was way before our time, of course,' her father told her, 'but there was something about May not being able to have children.'

'That's terrible!' Jess exploded. 'Derek loved May. I know he did. Surely he can't have wanted a family so much that he would sacrifice the woman he loved? Besides, how did she know she couldn't have children? In those days, there weren't any tests like today.'

'I don't know the whole story, but that's what May always told us. She didn't want to talk about it. She was deeply hurt and as you know, would have noting to do with that side of the family. Her parents left her the cottage and that made the rift even deeper.'

'So I gather. And then me inheriting it made things even worse.'

'How do you mean? Have you been in contact with someone, then?'

'I went to see June. She's in a nursing home. And I spoke to Julian, her son. He wasn't exactly friendly.'

'Goodness,' her mother said. 'You have been a busy bee, haven't you?'

'I was interested in the family story. I just wanted to know more.'

'Maybe you should leave it there.' Her father was looking a little nervous, Jess thought. Or was she just imagining that, knowing what she now knew?

'What made you to look these people up?' her mother said.

'I read some of May's letters. Did you realise she kept practically everything?'

'Come on, let's get back to the cottage and start supper. It's looking a bit like rain,' her mother said. 'We can have the pie I brought. It's chicken and mushroom. I do know you like my chicken pie, Jess.'

They were back on safer ground now and her parents were looking relieved.

They must have realised that she knew something of the truth from her comments about May keeping letters. Unless her father had forgotten what he had written all those years ago.

She needed to handle all this very carefully.

★ ★ ★

When they arrived back at the cottage, her mother busied herself with preparing the meal. 'Haven't you got a microwave, dear?' she asked. 'I thought May used one all the time.'

'I know. There used to be one, but I think it must have broken. Unless it was taken out by someone. Maybe my mysterious intruder decided to take it. Oh, look, the light's flashing again.' Jess pressed the button and the picture came up on the little screen.

'How weird. It looks a bit like May when she was younger. How she looked when we first knew her,' Jess's father said.

'I don't know how you can tell,' Jess responded. 'You can hardly see anything under the hood.'

'The way she holds her head. And look at her nose. That's May to a tee.'

'I think you may be right,' Sarah agreed.

'I hope you're not suggesting some sort of ghostly haunting!' Jess said.

'Course not! I suppose it couldn't be June, could it?' asked Bill thoughtfully.

'No. I told you, she's in a nursing home. She simply isn't capable of getting here, let alone wandering round the place. It must be someone who lives near. I've tried knocking on a few doors, but they all seem to be holiday lets and I haven't met anyone at all. Dan and his family don't know anything, either.'

'You said June had children? Do you know anything about them?'

'Only that she had two. A son, Julian. There was also a daughter, April.'

'So what about April? Could it be her? Perhaps she made it up with May and was used to coming here. Hence she knew where the coffee was.'

'It's possible, I suppose. She must be about sixty or so. She's older than Julian.'

'Supper's ready. Can you lay the table, please?' Sarah called from the kitchen.

After supper, her father said, 'I'd be really interested to see some of these old letters you mentioned.'

Jess frowned. Maybe this was the way she could introduce the subject of her parentage. If they saw the letters, it would show them what she knew. But May's letters from Derek, she would not let them see. They were too private and she intended to get rid of them as soon as she could.

'Okay. I'll bring one of the boxes down. If you're sure.'

★ ★ ★

Jess went upstairs and quickly looked through the boxes to find the one that contained her father's letters. She brought it down and set it on the now cleared table. She took out the bundle of letters which included her father's.

'You may be interested in some of these,' she said quietly, laying them down in front of her parents. Her father frowned slightly and picked up the envelopes with his writing. He glanced at his wife and then back at his daughter. She looked into his eyes, trying to fathom his thoughts. There was a sadness. A flicker of anxiety, perhaps.

'You know, don't you darling?' he said quietly.

'Yes, daddy. It was a big shock but somehow it seemed to explain some things.'

'I can't think what you mean Jess,' Sarah snapped. Jess bit her lip. She needed to be very careful what she said at this stage.

'Why didn't you tell me? I had the right to know. My father isn't my father at all. Not my biological father, anyway.'

'You couldn't have had any father who could love you more,' Sarah said hotly. 'It was his massive generosity that enabled you to be born at all. Can you imagine how he felt? He was forced to admit that he couldn't father his own child. He then had to stand by and wait for another man's child, the donor's child, to be born.'

Jess's eyes were filling with tears. It had been a terrible time for her parents and keeping it a secret all these years may not have been exactly the right thing to do, but she understood why they had done it.

'Mum, Dad, I'm sorry if I've upset you. Can you imagine the shock it was to me, though? To discover that the father I'd always loved wasn't my real father?'

'I suppose we hoped you've never find out,' her mother said. 'That you'd never need to know.'

'Do you know who my real father is?'

'No. It was all done anonymously.' Bill's voice shook with emotion. 'I suppose there might be some record somewhere. You're right, though. You do have the right to find out who your biological father is. We do know he looked quite like me.'

Her father looked stricken and couldn't meet Jess's gaze. She went over to him and put her arms round him.

'You'll always be my dad. Don't ever doubt it. And I do understand, now I've had time to get used to the idea.'

'But at first, I felt betrayed that you'd been lying to me all my life.

'I didn't know who I was any more.'

Both parents rose at exactly the same moment and put their arms round her.

'We couldn't love you more,' Bill said.

'I know, Dad. But I can't pretend I'll forget all about it. I'm sure I shall stare at people in the street and wonder.'

'There is one big thing that concerns me, though: I don't really have any right to this cottage. I'm not actually a blood relation of May.'

'Don't be silly. She wanted you to

have it,' her father said. 'You spent time with her and looked after her when she needed you. Besides, it's obvious she didn't want any of the rest of the family to benefit, especially when she had been treated so shamefully by her own sister.'

'Anyway, you're perfectly entitled to the cottage if it was May's wish. There's no obligation to keep it in the family.'

'Does Kim know anything about this?' Jess had to ask.

'No. She was far too young to know anything. And please don't ever mention it to her, will you?' Sarah looked troubled. 'Please, Jess. Can't we keep it our secret? I felt so devastated when I learned we weren't able to have any more children. Your father was heartbroken, feeling it was his failure. You were like a blessing Heaven-sent.'

'Oh, Mum.'

Tearfully, they clung to each other and Jess made up her mind there and then that this would be an end to it.

She didn't want to speak of her birth

again and upset her beloved parents any further.

Carefully, Jess replaced the letters in the box and took them upstairs. Maybe she should simply burn everything and forget what had happened. She knew she wasn't ever going to discuss it again. If she could clear her conscience about inheriting the cottage, then she would love to live here. She had come to love this place so much and would hate to lose it. Besides, there was Dan. If she couldn't move here, she would have to say goodbye to a man she knew was becoming very special to her.

The next morning, her phone rang. It was Dan.

'How's it going? Were your parents impressed?'

'Yes, everything's fine. I was going to call you and suggest you might like to come and meet them.'

'That's one reason I'm calling you. Mum insists that you bring them round for supper tonight, if you haven't made other plans.'

'That's very kind of her. I'll ask them and I can't believe they'll say no. They can't wait to meet you.'

'Heavens. What have you told them about me?'

'Only that you're tall, dark and handsome and good at decorating.'

'Handsome, eh? Now I am nervous.'

'You? Nervous? I don't believe that for one moment. What are you doing?' she asked, as a slightly odd noise sounded through the phone.

'It's Emily. She's getting impatient with me talking to another female.'

'I see. I'm sharing you yet again, am I?'

''Fraid so. Fact of life. If you had four legs and a tail, you'd get equal shares. But then, at least you can answer the phone when it rings. So maybe you're one up on the rest of my ladies.'

Jess laughed. 'That's nice to know. So what time this evening?'

'About six-thirty would be good.'

'Great. I'll call you back if there's a problem. I'm hoping Dad's going to make a start on the garden today. Once it's organised, I can keep it tidy. Except that I usually manage to keep the weeds and pull up the plants.'

'And I thought you were a biology teacher.'

'General science. Gardening wasn't included.'

'Look, I'd better go. I need to get back to the herd. See you later.'

Just then, her parents came back into the kitchen.

'Good morning, darling. Who were you talking to?' her mother said.

'It was Dan. Mrs Meadows has invited us round for supper this evening. I said yes, but I can call back if there's something else you'd rather do?'

'Of course not. That's really kind of her. We must get some chocolates for her.'

'Good idea. We can go to Penzance, if you like,' Jess suggested.

'I was rather hoping to make a start on the garden,' Bill protested.

'Mum and I can go and leave you to

it, if you like. Now, who's for some breakfast?'

They sat for a long time, enjoying coffee and large quantities of toast and Sarah's homemade marmalade. Then Bill went to investigate the gardening tools and Jess and her mother drove off to Penzance.

They wandered round the steep streets and breathed in the sea air by the car park on the quayside.

'It doesn't feel like proper shopping in a town like this, does it?' Sarah remarked. 'It's like being on permanent holiday. I'm glad you decided to move down here. I shall miss you terribly, but I think you'll have a much nicer life here.'

'I think so too,' Jess agreed. 'Providing I can get a job, of course. I expect everyone would like to live by the sea, so there'll be a lot of competition.'

They were going back to the car when Jess stopped suddenly. 'Goodness. Look at that girl. She could be my double. I wonder if she's Poppy, Julian's daughter?'

Without thinking, she rushed over to her. 'Poppy?' The girl turned and gave a start. 'You are Poppy, aren't you?'

'Yes. And you must be the person who inherited the family home. They said we look alike.'

'Jess. I'm Jess Cunningham. And this is my mother. It's nice to meet you.'

'I . . . er . . . I have to go. My parents warned me not to speak . . . Sorry, I must go.' She turned and fled up the street.

'Well, what do you make of that?' Sarah said to Jess.

'I assume her parents have told her to have nothing to do with me. I'm obviously not a welcome member of the family.'

'Don't start that again. You're perfectly entitled to inherit the cottage. If it upsets you, just keep out of their way.'

'I suppose. But I hate the thought of anyone disliking me so much. And you must admit, it's weird that we look so alike.'

A Mystery Solved

Bill had taken a good look round the garden to decide where exactly he should begin. May's once carefully tended flower beds were overgrown and full of weeds. It seemed that very little work had been done for many months. It must have been neglected well before May had died. He found a fork and wheelbarrow and began to dig out the weeds from a bed near the house when the little cat and her kittens arrived. Bill bent down to stroke them.

'Hello, where have you come from?' The cat walked down the path to the shed and he saw the empty dishes left out. 'So, you want something to eat, do you? My girl never mentioned she had a little family living in the shed. Let's see what we can find.'

He went into the kitchen and heard a noise coming from the sitting-room. 'Hello? You back already?' He pushed the door open and saw a slight figure standing in the hall. A hooded top was pulled down, partially covering the face. 'What . . . who are you? What are you doing in my daughter's house?'

'Ah, but she ain't your daughter is she? Not your proper daughter.'

'I don't know what you're talking about,' Bill said. He was shocked by the words, coming so soon after the revelations of the previous evening.

'You do. I can see it in your eyes. Didn't think anyone was here. Thought she'd left the door open by mistake. What's that horrible animal doing inside? Not clean, cats aren't. Bad enough when the old 'un had all them dogs. Messy things, dogs.'

'Who are you?' Bill said. 'Take your hood off so I can see your face. You're the one who's been taking things, aren't you? And hanging around the place?'

'Used to come and have a coffee with

171

the old 'un. Reg'lar it was. She never minded me having a cup of coffee. Did a few things for her, I did.'

'You mean you used to help her?'

'A bit. Didn't want any money for it.'

'Look, why don't I make you some coffee now? We can sit down and talk. You can tell me about yourself.'

'Not tellin'.'

'It's all right. I'll put the kettle on. Come into the kitchen.'

'Used to get in with the key. But that girl took it away. I didn't take anything that shouldn't have been mine by rights. Should have been our house, this one. My mum says so all the time.'

'I think you're April, aren't you? June must be your mother.'

'I'm not April. I'm Agnes, Agnes, Agnes. When I come here, I'm Agnes.'

Bill looked at the woman. Poor soul. She was more to be pitied than feared.

He made some coffee and put two large spoons of sugar into it.

'Make a nice cup of coffee, you do,' the woman said.

'So, do you live near here?'

'Up the lane. No . . . I don't. I don't know where I lives.'

'I see. And you see Jess, that's my daughter, you see her going out sometimes, do you?'

'Maybe. You got any biscuits? Likes a biscuit with my coffee, I do.'

'I'm not sure. I'll take a look.'

Bill opened the cupboard. There was some flapjack Sarah had made. 'I dare say you could have a piece of this.' He offered her the tin and she took out several pieces. She arranged them on the table and took a bite out of each one, as if making sure they remained hers.

'Nice.'

'So, April . . . Agnes, I mean. How long have you been coming here?'

'Lots of weeks.'

'Did you come and clear some weeds out one day?'

'She liked flowers. Only them dogs kept digging them up. Nasty messy things, dogs. Glad they went away.'

173

'And do you see your family sometimes? What about your mother? Do you see her?'

'I dunno where she's gone. Left me all on my own, she has.'

'And your brother? Julian, isn't it?'

'He don't want nothin' to do with me.

'His wife's too posh for our family. Thinks we're all crazy.'

'That's a pity. So what do you do with yourself all day?'

'Look after keys, I do. For them holiday places. I do collect laundry from them for when the laundry man comes in his van. He's nice, he is. Brings me chocolate sometimes.'

'Why did you say Jess isn't my daughter?'

'Saw it in them letters. I can read very well, I can. When the old 'un left here, I had a good look in her boxes of stuff. Load of junk if you ask me. Read some letters, though. Interestin' stuff in there. Some she hadn't even opened. I didn't open them. I didn't, honest.'

'Did May know who you were?'

'Nah. She wouldn't have let me in here if she'd known who my mum was. My brother was mad when the old 'un's will was read. Thought this place would come back into the family. Seein' his lawyer he is.'

Bill frowned as he contemplated the woman before him. Perhaps there was some family resemblance, but obviously not enough for May to have noticed it.

'For how many years were you visiting May?' he asked.

'Last couple of years. Since I moved into my flat. Gotta go now. Thanks for the coffee. I'll come again. But when that girl's not here. You're all right. You're family.'

'Wait. I don't know what you mean about Jess not being family. She's my daughter. Always has been.' But April . . . Agnes . . . wasn't listening. She had pulled her hood up and was already halfway out of the door.

★ ★ ★

175

Bill was concerned. April, or Agnes, had obviously been looking through May's old letters and seemed to have found out the truth about Jess's birth. He had hoped this would never come to light. Why had he confided in May and why on earth had she kept everything?

A curl of anxiety was winding itself round his heart. The old feeling of his inadequacy, stifled for so long, was rearing up inside him once more.

He cleared away the coffee cups. One mystery had been solved, but perhaps new problems were about to erupt.

He'd have to tell Sarah and Jess about his visitor when they got back. But should he mention her words that were now troubling him so deeply?

He went back outside, shutting the door carefully behind him. He began his weeding and allowed the peace of the garden to wash over him. There was always something calming about gardening, he thought. Something timeless and enduring.

* * *

By the time Jess and Sarah returned, he felt ready to tell them about the woman. 'So you see, the mystery is solved,' he concluded.

Jess and Sara had listened to his account open-mouthed.

'And she really is April?' Jess asked.

'Oh, yes, I'm certain. Though she's known as Agnes to everyone around here. I reckon she came here hoping to make some connection with May and possibly even to get the cottage back into her side of the family. But she's a confused lady and certainly not the brightest flower in the bunch. But the one troubling thing is that she knows about your parentage, Jess. She said something about Julian seeing a lawyer. That must be to contest the will. Mind you, she might not have a clue what she's talking about. Seems a bit confused.'

'How awful,' Jess said. 'Do you think they might have a case? I mean, to contest the will?' she asked worriedly.

'I doubt it. Unless May was not of sound mind when she wrote the will. And I don't think that was the case. She actually wrote the will several years ago. No, you needn't worry about it. I really don't believe there's any possibility there's anything dodgy. May would have been much too careful for that.'

'So I'm afraid I didn't get far with the gardening,' Bill confessed. 'I was interrupted quite early on. April, or Agnes, was actually inside the house when I discovered her. She lives in some sort of apartment, I gather. A key-holder for the holiday lets.'

'You must take care, love,' Sarah said anxiously to Jess. 'She might be a bit, well, unstable. I hate to think of you here on your own. Maybe you need to think twice about it all. Come back home and perhaps sell this place. It might give you a start on the housing ladder.'

'I've made up my mind, Mum. This

is where I want to be, I won't be intimidated. I may not feel happy about my inheritance in some ways but Auntie May wanted me to have this place and so I will. And if I have to fight a battle to keep it, so be it.'

* * *

As it was such a lovely afternoon, they all went outside to work in the garden. Jess was happy to be guided by her father and together they managed to tame a couple of overgrown flower beds. He made suggestions about planting shrubs that he knew would do well in the coastal conditions and they planned a trip to the local garden centre the next day.

'I'll buy them for you,' he said. 'Consider it a house-warming present.' He paused. 'Who's that leaning over the gate?'

Jess looked up. 'It's Dan. Hi, Dan. Come on in. Mum, Dad, this is Dan.'

They all shook hands rather formally.

Sarah was very interested in the young man in whose company her daughter had been spending so much time recently. She offered him tea.

'How can I refuse?' he said, glancing at Jess with a smile.

'I'll put the kettle on,' Jess said.

'Nonsense dear. You stay and talk to your guest.' Sarah went inside and busied herself with a tray and a tin of home baked goodies.

'You'll never stop your mother being in charge of anything to do with kitchens,' Bill laughed.

'So, what do you think of our efforts?' Jess asked Dan.

'Impressive. Is that cat still hanging around?' he said, spotting the little family romping around in the grass further down the garden.

'I meant to say,' Bill said. 'I gave them something this morning. They seemed to expect to be fed.'

'I haven't seen them for a while. They come and go. Dan doesn't approve of me feeding them. Says they're feral cats and should be left to fend for themselves.'

Dan put his arm round Jess and smiled down at her. 'As if anything I say would ever influence this one. She's quite something, this daughter of yours.'

'You don't need tell me. I'm very proud of her. Now, tell me about yourself. You farm next door, I gather?'

The two men chatted easily and Jess was interested to hear Dan talking in a way she hadn't really heard before. He told Bill he wanted to introduce new ideas and modernise some of their machinery, but his cautious father was rarely willing to take on major expenditure. And as long as his parents were still in charge, he had to bow to their wishes.

The tea arrived and the conversation took on a lighter tone. After chatting for a while, Dan excused himself to get back to the milking.

'You see how low in his priorities I am?' Jess said. 'Those other females have first call on his time.'

'Mum's looking forward to seeing you later,' Dan said. 'She's busy cooking a vast joint.'

'That sounds marvellous,' Bill said.

Sarah could hardly wait till Dan got through the gate before she began extolling his virtues.

'You should snap him up quickly,' she told Jess. 'He's gorgeous and your father likes him, I can tell.'

'Mum, really. He's a lovely man and I do like him. But don't go dropping hints about weddings all evening or I shall walk out, I promise you. I don't want him scared off by my pushy mum.'

'I'm not pushy. Just commenting that he's rather gorgeous.'

* * *

As it turned out, it was a most enjoyable evening. The two mums were soon swapping recipes and making veiled hints about their two offspring and how well they seemed to get on together. Bill and Dan's father chatted about the land and the difficulties of farming. Jess and Dan listened patiently then decided to go for a walk.

'I need to check on the stock and make sure all is well,' Dan had said, as they made their escape. The parents smiled knowingly.

'I bet they're planning our futures to the minutest detail,' Jess said with a grin, once they were out of the house.

'I guess. But tell me, how did it go with your dad? Did you tell him what you'd discovered? Was it all right? You all seemed pretty friendly.'

Dan's arm rested lightly round her shoulders in what had become a very easy manner. It felt comfortable there. Intimate but not intrusive in any way.

'It was okay. Fine, really,' Jess said. 'But they were both hurt that I'd found out the way I did.'

'Do you want children?' Dan asked suddenly.

'Well, yes, I suppose so. I haven't

given it a lot of thought. How about you?'

'Very much so. And if I thought you were totally set on a career and didn't want children, then I think I'd have to give a great deal of thought to where we're going.'

Jess felt her heart beating faster.

'And where are we going?' she said softly.

'Wherever you want. I think . . . maybe . . . ' Dan paused and the colour rose in his cheeks. 'I think . . . hope . . . that we might have a future together.'

'What are you suggesting?' She felt suddenly flustered and unable to find the right words.

'Nothing. Nothing. Sorry. Maybe I made a mistake. Maybe I'm jumping the gun a little . . . or a lot.'

'I don't think you were making any mistake,' Jess whispered.

'I was going to say that I love you.'

'I think I love you, too.'

'Only think?'

'No. I'm almost most certain I love you. It's all a bit too quick for me, though.'

'It's all right. I'm not asking for anything more at present. But if you think you might love me, that's fine. It's a start. I'm prepared to wait. Well, for a week, anyhow.'

'A week? Is that all?'

'Okay. Eight days. Only you'll be going back home soon and I don't want to let you go without a proper answer.'

'Remind me. What's the question?'

'Do you love me or only think you love me? Only there's quite a lot of competition. Eighty brown-eyed females all waiting for me to give them a glance.'

'Oh Dan . . . ' She could say no more. He pulled her into his arms and kissed her.

★ ★ ★

'So this is where you are. Everything all right, Dan?' His father sounded slightly embarrassed as Dan and Jess broke apart.

'Everything's fine,' Dan said.

His father looked back to the farm. 'I've been sent to fetch you. There's coffee on the go.'

When they got back, Mrs Meadows said, 'Getting on all right, you two, are you?'

'You could say that. Have you got all the wedding details sorted yet?' Dan said to his mother with a grin.

'Go on with you. What are you talking about?'

'I know you. You've been planning the marquee on the lawn since I was about five and kissed that girl from down the road.'

'Yet another female in your life, eh?' Jess teased.

'Oh dear,' Sarah murmured. 'You'd want a wedding here, wouldn't you? Only we have a lot of friends local to us.'

'Mum, for goodness' sake. What are you talking about?' Jess snapped. 'We're just joking. Having a laugh. Stop taking it all so seriously. We hardly know each other. If we ever do decide it's more than friendship, we'll let you know.'

Though Jess was almost certain she was in love with Dan, they would make their own decisions when they were good and ready.

'I'm going to walk down to the beach now,' Jess said. 'Thank you for a wonderful meal, Mrs Meadows.'

'I'll come with you, shall I?' Dan said.

'Better not, or they'll start planning the christening of our children.'

Dan looked hurt and Jess regretted her sharp comment. 'I'm sorry. Please, come if you'd like to.'

He took her hand and they walked through the meadow and down through the sand dunes to the beach. It was getting dark and the moon was glinting silver in a dark blue sky. It was still too bright to see any stars. The sea was lapping the shoreline making white frills at the edge of the sea.

'The crow black, sloe black, fishing boat bobbing sea,' Jess murmured.

'Under Milkwood?' Dan said, surprising her.

'Goodness, yes it is. I always loved it. Dad had a recording of it and he played it to us when we were little. Fancy you knowing it.'

'My dad had a recording of it and he used to play it when I was little,' countered Dan.

'Yes, Dan.'

'Yes what?'

'Yes, I do love you. Anyone who recognises a quote from Dylan Thomas has to be the right man for me.'

'Wow, that was easy.' He took her hands. 'Shall we forgive our mothers for making plans?'

'Dan, I don't want to think about anything more than us getting to know each other properly. We say we love each other but I'm not entirely sure I know what that means.'

'To me it means thinking of you every moment of the day. It means wanting to be with you. I simply can't imagine my life without you as part of it.'

'But you hardly know me. Not really.'

'Maybe not, but I know I love you. And it wasn't exactly love at first sight. I mean to say, it did take a couple of minutes.'

They laughed together as they walked across the sand, hand in hand, lost in each other and dreams of the future.

April Returns To The Cottage

Over breakfast the next morning, Bill made a list of the things he wanted to buy at the garden centre. Neither he nor Sarah had mentioned the previous evening and the unfortunate end when Jess had stormed off with Dan. They had returned to the cottage and Jess had come in some time after they had gone to bed. Her mother felt subdued and knew that, encouraged by Dan's mother, she had probably gone a little too far. Even the usually placid Bill had voiced his opinion. They had agreed not to mention the subject of weddings or the eminent suitability of Dan as a potential husband.

Inside, though, Sarah just knew Dan was the right one for her daughter and wondered how long she would have to wait for Jess to realise it for herself.

'We'd better go in my car,' Bill was saying. 'The boot's bigger and we have quite a lot to buy.'

'Mrs Meadows, Dan's mother, was saying they have a lot of bushes we can take cuttings from,' Sarah said. 'We had a bit of chat when you went off with Dan,' she told Jess. Bill shot her a warning glance and she said no more on the subject. But it was ridiculous, she thought: she couldn't just not mention the Meadows family for the rest of their stay.

★ ★ ★

They drove off, unaware of the woman watching from her window. When they were out of sight, she scuttled along the road and round to the back of the cottage. She rattled at all the windows, hoping to find a loose catch or somewhere left open. Finding nothing, she pulled a screwdriver out of her pocket and began to attack a window catch. She wanted to take another look at those letters. The ones that said this girl wasn't the man's daughter. That made her an outsider. No relation to the old 'un. Not entitled to the family home. Not that she had ever lived in the family home. The old 'un had lived there all her life and her own mother, June, had to live in rented accommodation. June would be pleased if she got it back. Might make her feel better about her daughter.

April had always been told she was stupid. Once her dad had died, there had been nobody to stand up for her and she had muddled on for many years, but June's sharp tongue had finally got her down and she had left home about five years ago. She had been given the job of caretaker to the holiday houses and lived in the small flat which went with the job. Since then, she had seen little of her family.

May had befriended her, though April had used a different name, hoping that the old 'un had no inkling as to who she really was. There had been trouble somewhere back in the past. April wanted to know what that trouble was. There must be something among all those letters the old 'un had kept. Her mother had once told her that she'd had a secret place in her bedroom when she'd been a little girl. April meant to discover it for herself. To find out the Big Secret from the past.

The window catch suddenly gave way and clattered to the ground. April pulled the window open and clambered inside, treading mud onto the clean floor.

★ ★ ★

'I don't even know what half these things are,' grumbled Jess as she inspected plant labels. 'Why do they have to have such complicated names?'

'Just look at the pictures, love, and then you can see what they look like,' her mother advised.

'Good thinking. I like those pinky

things and the purple ones. It says *seaside selection* so that must mean they'll grow around here. And I know that's heather.'

'A few plants from the heather family will certainly be a good idea,' her father said. 'Provide a variety of colours, too.'

Bill was enjoying himself. He'd always loved growing things and this was a chance to set up a new patch of garden exactly as he wanted. He knew that Jess might enthuse for the moment, but once she got a new job and was living here on her own, she would never show the same zeal for gardening. He estimated that if he and Sarah came down, say, twice a year, it would be enough to keep things tidy, especially if they used bark chippings for ground cover.

He was in his element and Sarah wandered off to look round the garden centre, leaving Jess feeling slightly uncomfortable as she pushed the trolley and watched her father load up with lots of expensive-looking containers. At last he was finished and went to the check-out.

Jess found her mother gazing at an array of conservatory furniture.

'I think some of this is gorgeous, don't you? It would look lovely in your lounge. Much better than those heavy old things of May's.'

'Gorgeous prices too, Mum. I have to watch my spending in case I don't get a job right away. I've already used up a stack of my savings.'

'I thought May left you some cash?'

'She did. But it hasn't come through yet. It's all tied in with inheritance tax and stuff. Besides, I don't expect it will be very much by the time everything's paid off and the solicitor's bill has been settled. Auntie May never had very much money around. I don't think she ever had a job, did she?'

'No idea. I don't think so. She was certainly very frugal, except when it came to her dogs. They always had the best of everything. Anyway, we'd better get back to your father or he'll be buying more plants.'

They loaded the car and set off for home.

'I can't let you pay for all this, Dad. It's far too much,' Jess said.

'I'm delighted to do it. I've always done things for Kim in her garden, so it's only fair. I bought them a load of plants when they moved to their new house, so I wanted to do it for you, too.'

★ ★ ★

'I'll sort lunch out while you unload the car,' Sarah said when they got back to the cottage. She let herself in through the back door and saw mud on the floor. 'Fancy Bill coming in here in his muddy boots,' she muttered. 'And we must have left the window open. Oh, glory. After all the problems Jess had with that strange woman, too. She just isn't responsible enough to live alone.' She went to the back door and called out, 'Jess! You left the window open and mud all over the floor.'

Jess came to look.

'I closed the window. I know I did.' She spotted the broken catch. 'Oh, no. Look here. It's been forced.'

'Get your father to call the police. They always take more notice of a man.'

'Rubbish,' Jess snapped, as she pulled out her mobile phone and punched in the number.

'Hello. I have to report a break-in. I think I know who's doing it and I'm not prepared to put up with it any longer.' She gave her address and said she would be in for the rest of the day. She closed the phone. 'They're sending someone round. Meanwhile, I have to see if anything's been taken.'

Sarah set about putting lunch together and Jess went upstairs. She gasped when she went into the little room where she had stored all May's boxes. Everything had been tipped out. There was also a panel pulled off the wall beside the bed. There was a cavity behind it and if there had been

197

anything inside it, it was now clearly empty.

Jess peered inside. It was a little secret hidey hole. The sort of place a child might hide away little treasures. Perhaps this had been May's room as a child, or even June's. The intruder must have been April again. She must have known about this cubby hole and had come to find something that had been hidden away, possibly for years.

Jess ran downstairs.

'I need a torch. I think there was one in one of the drawers,' she said.

'What's going on?' Sarah asked.

'There's a hole in the wall in the little room. Whoever broke in must have known it was there and has pulled the panel off. I can't see if there's anything still inside it.'

★ ★ ★

Jess ran back upstairs and shone the torch into the cubby hole. It was empty except for a scrap of paper. She pulled it out and stared at the faded writing. There was a heart drawn on the crumpled paper. *J.C. = D.W. True*, was written inside the heart. A typical teenage thing.

J.C. = D.W. June Cunningham equals Derek Wishart? He must surely have been engaged to May when June was a teenager. Or at least an older teenager. Jess looked into the hole again, but it was empty. If there had been anything else in there, it had now gone. She looked through the letters lying on the floor. The one which said that Bill was not her true biological father had gone.

What mischief was that woman plotting now?

She went downstairs and showed her mother the scrap of paper.

'I think it suggests that June was jealous of May right from the start of her relationship with Derek. Do you think she set out to take him for herself?' Jess asked.

'Maybe. But we shall probably never

know. Their secrets have gone forever into the past.'

'Maybe not. I shouldn't be surprised if there was something else in that hidden place. Something April found and took away.'

They discussed the possibilities over lunch. Bill remembered that the little room had been June's when she was a child. As the older daughter, May had had the larger room.

'My sister was always jealous of me,' May had told him. 'Used to say it wasn't fair that she was always second best.'

'So the little room with the secret cubby hole had been June's room. I reckon she must have told April about it and she came to search it while we were out,' Jess said. 'I wonder what she intends to gain by all of this?'

★　★　★

They had just finished coffee when a police car drew up outside the gate.

'Oh, dear,' Jessica said. 'I wonder what I should say to them? It seems a bit awful to tell them about April. I don't really want to get her into trouble, but I can't go on having her break in whenever she feels like it.'

The constable who had been previously, knocked on the door.

'More bother is it, ma'am?' he said to Jess.

'I'm afraid so. We think we know who it is, though, and while we don't want to get her into trouble, I can't allow her to keep breaking in. She broke the window catch this time.'

'You'd better give me details of this person. I suppose you know where she lives?'

Jess and her parents told their tale and the constable noted down the details.

'What I suggest is that I call on this lady. I'll take her to the station to help with enquiries, and maybe that will scare her sufficiently to stop her little games.'

'We're worried about our daughter living here on her own,' Sarah said. 'And then the place will be empty for a while until she moves down here permanently.'

'I can understand. Bit remote down here, isn't it? But at least you've got the Meadows family living pretty close. I take it you know them?'

'Oh, yes, very well. In fact, Dan . . . ' Sarah caught the warning glance from both Jess and Bill. 'In fact, Dan has set up a security monitor for Jess,' she said, glaring back at her husband and daughter.

*　*　*

Jess saw the policeman off.

'Hey, Jess. Is everything all right?' a voice called from the lane.

'Oh, hi there, Dan. Yes, we're fine.'

'Only I saw the police car here.'

'Our friend has been visiting again. She forced the window catch and then ransacked all May's documents as well

202

as pulling a panel off the wall. We think she may have taken something from a sort of secret cubby hole. Something of June's maybe. I'd love to know what it was. It might have given us some clues about the rift between May and her sister.'

'Interesting. So, am I allowed to kiss you?'

'I don't see why not.'

'It is broad daylight and your parents are nearby.'

'So?'

'Wow. You have become uninhibited all of a sudden.'

'Maybe I can't resist your charms.' They kissed and Jess felt happy and safe. 'You'd better come and say hello to your greatest fan. Mum will never forgive me if I don't take you inside. Do you want a coffee?'

'No, thanks, I have to get back to my other females. But I will say hello to your parents.'

Hand in hand, they went into the house. Bill was outside, planting his bushes and heathers. He gave them a wave as they passed and continued his work. He wanted to get as many plants into the ground as possible over the next couple of days and he wanted the job done without wasting time on idle chat.

Sarah was quite the opposite. She wanted to talk for as long as Dan would stay and listen.

She questioned him about his life and his plans for the future.

'Mum, leave the poor man alone. He has cows to milk and he really doesn't need your version of the Spanish Inquisition,' Jess said.

'Sorry, just interested,' Sarah said. 'You will thank your parents again for a lovely evening, won't you? It was a splendid meal. We'd like to return their hospitality before we go. Can we take you all out for dinner, perhaps? Jess says the pub in the village isn't bad. We could go tomorrow if that suits. We plan to head home the next day. Give Jess some space before she has to come back to start her new term.'

'So soon?' Dan said.

'It was really only a flying visit to check things out and see how Jess was coping.'

But it was not Bill and Sarah's return home which had saddened Dan.

'I'll ask my parents about a meal,' he said. 'Dad hates eating out but he did seem rather taken with you all. He might break the habit of a lifetime. See you later.'

Jess went to help her father in the garden. Bill had planted several of the shrubs and was now mixing in compost to the soil before planting some perennials. He had decided on putting the heathers all together in a bed near the house so there would be colour all year round. There were several large rocks lying around the garden and he and Jess struggled to carry them to the heather bed and place them among the plants. They stood back to admire their efforts just as Sarah came out with a tray of tea.

'Thought you might do with a break. I say, that looks really lovely. Once the plants have bushed out a bit, it will be perfect.'

'I'm rather pleased with it too,' Jess agreed. 'Shouldn't take too much looking after.'

They worked on until all the plants were in the ground.

'We need to get some bark chippings to act as mulch and if we put a weed mat down, too, that should help keep it all tidy.'

'You've done enough already, Dad,' Jess said. 'Maybe Dan will know someone who can supply bark chippings. He seems to know where to get most things.'

Sarah smiled happily, but managed to restrain herself from commenting. The more excuses her daughter could find to spend time with Dan, the better she would like it. Would he come to live with her in the cottage once they were married? she fantasised. Or would his parents want to hand over the farm to them? Perhaps they would live in the cottage and Jess and Dan would have the farm.

'Mum? What on earth are you planning now? You were miles away.'

'Nothing, darling. Just thinking about the future and where you might . . . work.'

'That reminds me. I must get a local paper. See if there are any jobs going.'

'Shall I walk up to the village to get a paper?' her mother offered.

'If you don't mind. Thanks. We'll finish off out here and then I need a shower.'

Sarah set off. It was a little way to the shop but it was a sunny afternoon and she enjoyed the chance to look in the various gardens as she passed. She noticed the police car outside one of the holiday homes and peered up the drive to see what was going on. The constable who had visited them earlier was knocking on a door at the rear. Presumably it led to the flat where April lived. She slowed down, hoping to see what happened but nobody was answering and the policeman turned away. He saw her and came over.

'The woman you suspected of breaking in to your daughter's cottage seems to be out. I've been here twice but there's no reply. I shall try again later. You don't know of anywhere she might be, do you?'

'Not really. Unless she's visiting her mother. She's in a nursing home somewhere. My daughter knows.'

'I'll give it one more try later and then maybe come and see you again. Thanks.'

* * *

Sarah continued her walk. She pushed open the door of the village shop. 'Good afternoon. I'm Jess's mum, Sarah. Jess Cunningham at May's old cottage? You might have met her?' she said to the shopkeeper.

'Afternoon, Mrs Cunningham. How's your girl settlin' in?'

'Fine, thanks. I hoped to buy a copy of the local paper. Do you have one?'

'Only last week's, I'm afraid. We do have the Western Morning News, if that's any good.'

'I'll take last week's and the Morning News, thanks.'

'I see the police have been down your lane. Know what that's all about?' asked the shopkeeper.

'I really couldn't say,' Sarah replied. 'Now, what do I owe you?'

She paid up and made her escape.

Jess quickly scanned the job pages of the two papers. Being late summer, there was very little available. It was the wrong time for teaching posts to be advertised.

★ ★ ★

Sarah told Jess about her conversation with the policeman.

'I wonder if April has gone to see June?' Jess mused.

'I wondered that myself. I said as

209

much to our policeman, but I'd no idea where the nursing home is, so I couldn't help.'

'Maybe I should go there again and see if I can find out anything more.'

They all felt weary after their efforts in the garden and had an early night. Jess lay awake, contemplating the future. She was secure and happy in the knowledge that Dan was going to be a big part of her life.

Her mobile rang.

'What are you doing?' Dan asked.

'Actually, I was thinking about you. Dan, how can you be so sure about us? You don't even know things like my favourite colour. What music I like. What food I like. The list is endless.'

'Ah, but I do know your favourite colour. It's blue.'

'How do you know that?'

'You wear blue a lot. And blue is the predominant colour of the things you bought for your room.'

'Hmm. You're too observant by far.'

'Better get some sleep now. 'Night, my love.'

''Night Dan.' He disconnected his phone and she whispered, 'Love you.' He didn't hear.

★ ★ ★

Over breakfast next morning, Sarah said, 'I thought we might spend some time on the beach today. What do you think?'

'We could have a walk, I suppose, but I'd hoped to finish things off in the garden,' Bill said.

'I think you've worked quite hard enough for one week. If you're really going home tomorrow, you should relax,' Jess told him.

They all agreed on a walk to the beach later and Bill went to do a little more in the garden.

Jess's mobile rang.

'Hi gorgeous. How are you this morning?'

'Hi, Dan. I'm fine. We're going for a

walk on the beach in about an hour or so.'

'I might join you. I'm just calling about your mother's invitation for supper this evening. My parents have agreed to try the food at the pub. I have to say, it's a first. Our parents must have enjoyed each other's company.'

'Or they want to gang up on us to admit we have something going.'

'Maybe. Do we? Have something going?'

'Oh I think you can safely say that. Besides, I need someone in my life who knows about bark chippings.'

'Now there's an invitation.'

Jess laughed. 'See you later.'

Amazing News

That evening, both families chatted easily and shared a very pleasant time.

'That was very good. Thank you for inviting us. We'll do it again next time you're down here,' Dan's father said. 'Now, if you'll excuse us, I think it's time I called it a day. I'll do the milking tomorrow, Dan, so you can have a bit of a lie-in.'

'Thanks, Dad, that would be great. So, do you fancy a drive somewhere, Jess?'

'Well, it is Mum and Dad's last night. Maybe I should go back with them.'

'Don't be silly. We shall go straight to bed when we get in. Early start for us tomorrow, too. You go and enjoy yourselves,' Sarah said.

'We could go to that new club in

Penzance, if you like,' Dan said. 'I'm not sure what music you like but it could be a chance to find out.' Dan had a definite twinkle in his eye as he spoke.

'What sort of music is it?' Jess asked.

'Wait and see.'

★ ★ ★

Their parents walked back along the lane together, the fathers talking about gardening and the mothers discussing their offspring. 'You must be so proud of her, she's such a lovely girl, and so level-headed,' Mrs Meadows said.

'And your Dan, too. So reliable and responsible. It must be a great comfort for you to know he'll manage the farm for you and do it so well.'

When they finally parted, they all promised to keep in touch.

Meanwhile, Dan and Jess had arrived at the club and stood outside listening to the noise erupting from inside.

'What do you think?' Dan said.

'I don't think that's my sort of music

at all,' Jess told him.

'Thank goodness for that. I hate it, too. I only suggested it to see if I could discover a little more about you. Crash course in learning about Jess. So, where do we go now?'

'We could walk round the harbour.'

'Sounds good to me. A woman who prefers walking to clubbing. Can't be bad.'

'Hey, isn't that my double over there?' Jess said suddenly. 'Isn't that Poppy, Julian's daughter?'

'You're right. I'm sure she's the one I thought was you that time.'

'Quick, let's catch up with her. Poppy! Poppy!' Jess called.

The girl stopped and turned. 'Oh it's you. I thought I'd made it plain that I didn't want to talk to you.'

'But why? This family feud, well isn't it about time we talked about it? Maybe you know what it was all about. I certainly don't, but I'd like to find out. Why don't we have a drink somewhere. Is there a coffee place open still?'

'Well . . . okay,' Poppy said, and looked approvingly at Dan. 'Aren't you going to introduce me to your man?'

'Sorry. This is Dan Meadows.' The two shook hands and Poppy held on for a moment too long, in Jess's opinion.

'Not *the Dan Meadows*? Local hero and winner of all the regattas?' Poppy gushed,

'When I was a kid. I haven't sailed much since.' Dan was blushing and looked rather uncomfortable.

'And you live at the farm behind her cottage?' Poppy managed to make the *her* sound slightly unpleasant.

Dan nodded.

'So, what do you think of the music?' Poppy nodded towards the club. 'Pretty cool eh?'

'Actually, it's not exactly our scene,' Jess said.

'Mmm. That figures.'

They walked toward the harbour and found a little café.

'So, what do you want to know?' Poppy said.

'Do you know why May and her sister, your gran, fell out so badly?' Jess asked.

'Granny June would never speak of it,' Poppy said. 'She claimed she tried to make up, but May always rejected her olive branches. She told us she had written to May but she'd never had the courtesy of a reply.'

'May never read the letters. I found them unopened in one of her boxes,' Jess said, and then added, 'What do you know about your aunt? April?'

'April? She's a bit, well, a bit short on the brain side of things. She's got worse over the years. I think she's got a job somewhere with a flat or something. We haven't seen anything of her since I went to college. I only went locally. We couldn't afford for me to go to University properly. We were always the poor side of the family.'

'I'd like to meet your father,' Jess said. 'Do you think he would see me?'

'Doubt it. He's just as bitter about you inheriting as ever.'

They talked in a somewhat restrained way for a few more minutes and then Poppy said she had to get home.

'Can we drop you somewhere?' Dan offered. He'd been silent for most of the time.

'It's okay. I only live a few minutes walk away. Do touch base with me if you're ever at the club again.'

She was clearly offering the invitation to Dan, but Jess couldn't resist replying, 'Oh, we will. Certainly we will. The next time we're at the club we'll look out for you.'

'What a charmer,' she muttered as Poppy left. 'And what was all that sailing hero stuff about? *The* Dan Meadows indeed. And I'm no nearer the solution of the great rift.'

'Almost certainly June was jealous of her sister and set out to steal her man. Somehow, she managed to capture him.'

'Derek was still in love with May, though. I told you I found love letters from him till right up to his marriage.

Oh, look, let's forget about all this for now and go for our walk.'

* * *

They walked hand in hand by the harbour. Lights reflected against the water, dancing gold showers of movement between the moored boats. A little further away, there were lights shining down from the castle on St Michael's Mount, out in the bay.

'This is such a beautiful place. How can anyone really leave Cornwall behind them? Even if you have to go away, there will always be a part of it left deep inside,' Jess said.

'I'm so glad you feel that way,' Dan told her. 'And I don't want you to go away, ever.'

'Nor me. But there's no way round it. I have to work my notice. So, Dan, tell me about these sailing exploits of yours.'

'It was nothing really. Just a few local regattas when I was a lad.'

'You offered me a trip out in your boat, remember,' Jess said.

'Which you turned down.'

'Ask me again,' she said happily.

★　★　★

Jess saw her parents off soon after breakfast the next morning. It would be just over a week before she returned to them, ready to begin her next term at school.

The sailing trip was planned for the rest of the day and lunch was to be included at a little harbour along the coast. Jess had sailed only a couple of times before on school outings, but she was a good swimmer and had no fear of the water. Besides, Dan was an expert.

She locked up carefully and checked all the windows. The broken catch had been replaced and the new one included a lock. But she doubted if April would be back.

She had found what she had been looking for on her last visit.

* ★ *

Jess walked down the path to the Meadows' farm. There was quite a breeze this morning. Perfect for sailing, according to Dan.

Down at the beach, they uncovered the little sailing dinghy. The mast was folded down and the vessel looked rather neglected.

'I haven't been down here for ages,' Dan confessed. 'I'll need to put up the sails and check everything before we go. Sorry. I should have realised it might need a spot of maintenance.'

'What can I do to help?' Jess asked.

'There's a bucket and tap over there. Clean water would be good.' He began to check the various ropes and cleats until he was satisfied that all was well.

Jess washed out the bottom of the boat and watched as the water trickled out of two flaps at the back. 'Doesn't the water leak into the boat through those?' she asked.

'No. The water pressure is greater

outside than in. We can sometimes open the transom flaps to let the water out when we're going fast enough. If we've shipped too much, that is.'

'Now I'm beginning to feel nervous,' she laughed.

'No need. I know what I'm doing. Now, can you help me get the trailer down to the water? Shouldn't be too heavy.'

'What about the mast and everything?'

'Need to get her afloat before we put that up. Okay. That's it. Don't get your shoes wet. Nothing worse than sailing in soggy shoes.'

Once the boat was afloat, Dan climbed in easily. 'Do you think you could manage to pull the trailer back up the beach?' he said to Jess.

Jess heaved the trailer up the beach. It wasn't easy going when she reached the softer sand, but with the help of a holiday-maker, they got it high enough to be out of danger of the incoming tide. She thanked the man and ran back down the beach. Dan already had the mast raised and was busy threading on the sail.

'Thanks for that. You can get in now, if you like.'

'How do I get over the side?'

'Okay. I'll get out and help you. I take it you haven't sailed before?' Dan's blue eyes twinkled.

'Only on a lake,' Jess said. 'And there was a landing stage. All I had to do was step into the boat very gracefully.'

Dan held the boat still for her. She flopped over the side and landed on the bottom in an untidy heap. 'Not a lot of grace in evidence there,' Dan laughed. 'Are you all right?'

'I'll survive.'

'Put on this life jacket. Then you can just sit and enjoy the breeze while I pull up the sails. The boat will top the other way to where you're sitting, so be ready.'

Jess clung to the side of the boat, bracing herself for the movement. As soon as the wind filled the sails, Dan expertly turned the boat to minimise the tilt. He settled the ropes, which he said were called sheets, and set the helm out to sea. They bounced over the breakers and were soon in calmer water. Jess still felt tense but the wind rushing through her hair made her feel a sense of freedom she had never known before. She began to relax and look around her. They were going at quite a pace and a feeling of exhilaration was filtering into her.

'I love you Dan,' she yelled. He grinned and mouthed back *and me*.

★　★　★

'Do you want to have a go at the helm?' Dan offered. 'You can sit close to me and I'll help you.'

'You mean actually move around in this rocking, heaving little craft? Actually stand up?'

'Come on. It's quite safe.'

'Can I try it next time? I'm really not ready yet.'

Dan shrugged and looked disappointed. Jess felt bad, but it was no use doing something she wasn't ready for.

Soon, they were back in their own cove. When they were close to the shore, Jess slipped off her shoes and climbed over the side. She held the boat steady as Dan pulled down the sails and lowered the mast.

'Well done. You're learning fast. If you hold on, I'll go and collect the trailer.'

She watched as he ran up the beach and pulled the boat trailer back, as if it weighed nothing at all. Her heart thumped as she watched him. How would she bear it when she had to leave him?

Together, they dragged the boat on to the trailer and began the long haul up the beach. At last they reached the spot where the boat stayed permanently. 'That's me done for the day,' Jess said, flopping down on the sand.

'Sorry, but I have to get back,' Dan said. 'You know. The cows. Oh, and

Mum said you were to come back for supper. With your parents gone, she thinks you'll feel lonely and probably never eat again.'

'That's so kind. I really shouldn't keep coming round like this, though.'

'I shouldn't try to argue. Mum usually gets what she wants.'

'Thank you then. Yet again. I'll go back home and shower and change. Make sure all is well. No more intruders or anything.'

* * *

He kissed her as she left him outside the farm. She smiled happily and walked back to the cottage, where all seemed well.

There were several envelopes lying on the mat. A couple of bills, some junk mail and two letters from two different solicitors.

One was from May's solicitor and Jess ripped this envelope open first.

Dear Miss Cunningham,

In connection with the estate of your late aunt, Miss May Cunningham, I am pleased to inform you that probate on the estate is now completed and after payment of all taxes and expenses due, the residue of one hundred and twenty thousand pounds and fifty eight pence can be paid to you on receipt of your bank details.

Jess gasped. Over a hundred thousand pounds? She couldn't believe it. More than that, she couldn't accept it. And how had her aunt amassed so much money? She had always lived so frugally. Even her parents were unaware of how much money May had and shared her belief that the money was gong to be, at most, a few hundred pounds.

Jess sat down and felt the tears welling in her eyes. Poor May. How generous she had been. And whatever had happened in the past, her close family should receive something. Jess made up her mind to share her good fortune.

She picked up the other letter from another Penzance solicitor. Instantly, her mood changed. It was from a company acting on behalf of Julian Wishart and family in pursuing the contesting of the will of the late May Cunningham. They were attempting to prove that May was not of sound mind when the will was made in favour of Jess. They accused Jess of taking advantage of a sick, confused old lady to persuade her to leave her entire worldly possessions to her.

Tears of hurt and anger filled Jess's eyes. It was all nonsense, of course. The whole business had come as a great surprise to her and she had never even seen Aunt May again after that one summer. If she had been guilty of coercing her aunt, it had taken a mighty long time for her to change her will.

She wanted to tell someone and thought of Dan. But he was working. She glanced at her watch. It was already almost five o'clock. She dialled the number of May's solicitor and waited as it rang out for what seemed like ages.

A New Life Beckons

To Jess's relief, someone answered the phone. 'Blakes and Jenkins, how can I help?'

'Can I speak to Mr Blakes please? It's rather urgent.'

'Who's calling?' Jess gave her name. 'I'll see if he's still in his office.' Jess sat chewing her nails. There were several clicks and eventually she heard the solicitor's voice and breathed a sigh of relief. She quickly told him about the contents of the letter.

'They're trying it on. Don't worry, they don't have a leg to stand on. I've known May for years. She decided to cut the family out of her Will long ago, well before she even knew you. There was a lot of history, of which you may or may not be aware. After your kindness to her when she was ill, she decided to leave everything to you, her niece.'

Jess took a deep breath.

'Actually,' she began, 'I'm not really her niece. I am not my father's biological daughter. I never knew this until I was going through Aunt May's things and found a letter from my father. April, Julian's sister, discovered this and stole the letter. I suppose they think this gives them grounds to contest the Will.'

'Anyone can leave anything to anyone they choose,' Mr Blakes said. 'I fully believe there is no case to answer, but I suggest you come into the office first thing on Monday. Don't worry, Jessica, we shall sort it out for you.'

'Thank you so much. I was planning to give the family some of May's money anyway. It was far more than I was expecting.'

'I trust you will reconsider your plans. May was adamant that her family should receive nothing.'

'But why was she so antagonistic

towards them all?'

'I'll tell you what I know when you come into the office. In the meantime, don't worry.'

'Thank you. I'll see you on Monday, Mr Blakes.'

She dialled her parents at home. They should be there by now. There was no reply but she left a message, asking them to call her. It was a worrying time, despite the reassurance of the solicitor. She couldn't bear to lose this lovely cottage.

A thought struck her. With all May's money behind her, she needn't worry about finding a job immediately. She could hand in her notice and look for something when she moved down permanently. It still didn't get her out of having to go back to serve her notice, though.

★ ★ ★

Jess's mobile rang as she was walking to Long Meadows. It was her mother.

'Is everything all right?' Sarah asked.

'I think so,' Jess replied. 'I had a letter from the solicitor to say that Aunt May has left me over one hundred thousand pounds. Can you believe it?'

'Oh, darling, how simply wonderful. What a start in life she's given you. Bill, guess what?' Jess listened as her mother told her father the news.

'Mum? That's not all. I also had a letter from another solicitor to say that Julian and his family are trying to contest the Will on the grounds that May was of unsound mind and that I persuaded her to change her will in my favour.'

'What rubbish. You must get to the solicitor first thing on Monday.'

'I already did. He says there's nothing to worry about but I am seeing him on Monday. But Mum, The Wisharts know about the circumstances of my birth. You know . . . about Dad and everything.'

'This is all that wretched woman April's doing. I wish we'd pressed charges against her for the burglaries now. Are you seeing Dan tonight? You shouldn't be alone.'

'I'm on my way to the farm right now.'

★ ★ ★

It seemed a long weekend. Jess tried to enjoy her time with Dan, but her mind kept drifting back to her meeting with the solicitor on Monday. Dan suggested another sail, but she really wasn't in the mood. They did take a picnic lunch on Sunday and walked for miles over the headland towards Lands End. It began to rain soon after they had eaten, and both got soaked as they were a long way from the car. Jess sneezed and complained that a cold was all she needed now.

★ ★ ★

On Monday morning, Jess was waiting outside the office when Mr Blakes arrived.

'Sorry to call so early but I was a bit, well, a lot, anxious.'

'Come in. I'll organise some coffee and we'll see what we can sort out.'

Once they were settled in Mr Blakes' office, he perched some half moon glasses on his nose.

'I take it this business is true? About your parentage, I mean?' he said.

'Yes. But he is my dad and always will be. May was his cousin, so you see, I'm not really a direct relation.'

'As I said, that doesn't matter at all. And I can assure you that May's mind was perfectly sound when she made her will in your favour. And it was some time after your visit. Two years or more, so any coercion simply could not be proved. No, Jessica, you have nothing to fear from the legal side. I shall write to Julian Wishart on your behalf and let's hope there's an end to it.'

'Do you know where May got all her money from? I was amazed she left so much.'

'There were some bonds she had

bought many years ago. I suspect they had been forgotten, but they turned out to be a good investment. They paid the inheritance tax and all the expenses.'

They chatted for a few moments longer and Jess left. As she walked away, she remembered the solicitor needed her bank details and turned back. Someone called out to her. It was Poppy.

'Poppy. What are you doing here?' Jess said.

'Waiting for you. I saw you going into those offices. I need to talk to you. Can we get a coffee somewhere?'

'I suppose so. I take it you know about your father's actions to try and disinherit me?'

'I know, yes. He told me about it. Some idea of making it up to me for not sending me to university. Truth is, I'm not clever enough anyway. I got a job in Plymouth for a while but I hated living away from Cornwall.'

They went into one of the many coffee bars and sat down. It was still early and not many people were around. Poppy kept glancing towards the window.

'Are you expecting someone?' Jess asked.

'Not really. It's just that, well, I don't want to be seen talking to you.'

'Consorting with the enemy, you mean! Well, you may as well know that I've been to see a solicitor and he assures me that your family have absolutely no chance of winning their case. May was of sound mind when she wrote her Will and it was two years after my stay, so coercion is not an issue either. If you have any control over your parents' actions, I'd suggest you advise them to stop now or they could lose a lot of money in legal fees. No solicitor comes cheap these days.'

'I doubt they'd listen to me. I heard talk of May having some money, which I suppose you got as well?'

Jess didn't reply.

'I guess that's a yes. The thing is, I want to start a business and need some capital. I might be able to persuade my father to drop his claim on the cottage if you can see your way to finance me. Come on. You can afford a few thousand.'

Jess's temper flared. 'You really are a piece of work, aren't you? I don't know how you have the gall to ask for money after all you've put me through.' She gave a wry laugh. 'I was actually thinking I might make a gift to your family but my solicitor was adamant that would be contrary to May's wishes.'

Poppy immediately became contrite. 'Please, Jess,' she begged. 'I can't bear to go on living with my parents. Maybe you'd like someone to share your cottage? We could go into business together. Be partners.'

'No, Poppy. Besides . . . ' she paused. She had been on the verge of saying she was going to be away for the next few months and realised this would be stupid. Goodness knows what they would get up to if they knew the cottage was empty. 'I have other plans,' she finished. 'Now, I'll just pay for the coffees and get on. Goodbye.'

She left the café and went back to the solicitors to give her bank details. She asked if she could see Mr Blakes again and was shown into his office. She told him about Poppy's approach for money.

'Don't even think about giving her anything,' he said. 'I've told you, they have no claim on May's estate. You didn't tell her about the money, did you?'

'No, but she knew there was money. Maybe April found out about that, too.'

'I think you might need to take out a restraining order on that woman,' Mr Blakes said. 'She could be banned from coming near you.'

'I'll think about that. But I should install a proper alarm system. I shall be away from the place for some months until I can get down here permanently.'

'Then you certainly must.'

'You said you knew something of the family rift?' Jess ventured.

'I was told in confidence but I expect, as May's beneficiary, she wouldn't mind you knowing after all this time.'

'You know she was engaged to be married to Derek Wishart?'

Jess nodded.

'It seems June did all she could to take Derek away from her sister and get him for herself. There were many incidents and finally she told everyone she was pregnant by him. In those days it was a great scandal and her parents forced them into marriage. Derek was totally innocent, but at May's insistence, he went ahead and married June to save the family from disgrace.'

'So who was the father?'

'She was never pregnant. It was all a lie.'

'I can't believe anyone would do such a thing. Why did Derek go along with it? He clearly loved May. There were love letters to her right up to the week he married her sister.'

'You have to understand the scandal

of unmarried mothers in those days. A huge stigma. Any respectable family, especially in Cornwall, couldn't live with the ruin of the family's reputation. And May's father was very strict.'

'Poor May. And poor Derek. But at least he and June had some life together. Two children of their own.'

'Well, I suppose so. June was always a very strong lady. She got what she wanted most of the time.

'Now,' the solicitor went on, 'your money should be in place by the end of the week. I'll let you know the outcome of my letter to Julian Wishart.'

★ ★ ★

Jess went back to her car and drove to the supermarket. Her mind was going round and round, thinking about everything she had been told. It seemed ridiculous to her that June could have got away with her lies.

Dan called when she got home. She told him the latest news and about her encounter with Poppy. He was horrified and made her promise not to contact any of the Wisharts ever again. 'I'll be round in ten minutes,' he added.

They sat in the garden and chatted through the morning's events again. Jess mentioned her thoughts of resigning immediately she went back and looking for a job when she moved down.

'May's money means I'll be independent for a long time. It also means I can afford to have a proper security system put in. Something that alerts the police station if anyone breaks in.'

'Very wise. I'll keep a lookout, of course, but I'm not around that often. Now, I've got about three hours spare. Any ideas of what you'd like to do?'

'I really should sort out this security.'

'Do that tomorrow morning while I'm working. I want you to myself for a bit. Do you fancy another sail? It's not too windy and you might even have a go at taking the helm.'

'Okay. That would be nice.'

241

They called at the farm and Dan's father offered to do the milking so they could spend more time together. They accepted gratefully and within an hour they were sailing over the water towards the open sea.

Tentatively, Jess slid along her seat until she was close to Dan and nervously took the rudder from him.

Immediately, the sails flapped wildly.

'It's okay. Turn it slightly towards me and hold on to the mainsheet.' Dan's arm went protectively round her and together they managed to make progress. It was rather nice to feel his strong arms protecting her.

'I think I'd like you to take over now,' she said after a while. 'The wind seems to be getting up.'

'You're right. Bit of a squall. You often get them on this bit of the coast. I'll turn round. Ready?' He manoeuvred the boat, the sails swung round and they turned. But somehow, Jess lost her balance and ended up sprawled in the bottom of the boat. 'Sorry, love, are you all right? I thought you realised which way the boat was going. Jess? Are you all right?' Dan said.

'No,' she whispered. The pain was excruciating. 'I think I might have broken my arm.'

'Oh Heavens, I'm so sorry. I'll get us back as quickly as I can. Can you get up?'

'No. I daren't move.'

'I can't let go of anything to help you. I'm so sorry.'

★ ★ ★

Jess lay in the bottom of the rocking boat wishing she was back on dry land. She began to feel queasy and lifted her head to see how far from land they were. It looked like miles.

'Just hang on in there,' Dan said, 'I'll keep it as steady as I can but I need to catch the wind. It's really blowing quite hard at the moment.'

It was the longest twenty minutes she had ever lived through. Skilfully, Dan manouevered the little craft through the choppy waves, looking anxiously at Jess as the beach came closer.

As soon as they were near to land, he dropped the sail, warning her to keep her head down as the nylon fabric billowed down into the boat. He leapt over the side and dragged the boat as far onto the beach as he could. He dug the anchor into the sand and reached in to help Jess out. 'Oh, my love, I'm so sorry. I haven't even got my phone with me. Do you want to stay here while I run back and call an ambulance?'

'I'd rather try to walk. It might help clear my head. But what about the boat?'

'I need to get you sorted first. The tide's still going out. It'll be fine where it is for a bit. I'll get one of the sailing crowd to move it if need be. Come on, now. Take it steady. Lean on me.'

They walked slowly up the beach. Jess felt weak and sick. Halfway up, she needed a rest and Dan carefully helped her to sit down on a large rock. He pulled his tee-shirt off and made a sling for her arm. 'Stay there a minute. Don't try to move.'

He loped off to a crowd of young men and spoke to them. He pointed at his boat and a couple of them nodded and went down towards it. Another handed him a mobile phone. He went back to Jess. 'Ambulance on its way. Those two are going to put the boat away for me. They'll pack the sails and drop them round to the farm later.'

'I'm sorry. I was careless,' Jess said.

'Don't be silly. I'm the one who's sorry.'

'But if my arm's broken, however will I drive home next weekend?'

'You won't. You might just have to stay here.'

'How can I? What about my job?'

'You'll have to take sick leave.'

* * *

Over three hours later, Dan was driving Jess back to the farm. She had a plaster cast on her arm and a supporting sling. It was her right arm and as she was right-handed, she was very worried about how to cope for the next few weeks. She knew her mother would offer to come and help, but it wasn't fair to her. Alternatively, she could somehow return home and stay with them. It was a dilemma.

Mrs Meadows insisted she stayed with them overnight, just until she felt a little better. Jess, though, insisted on returning home the next day and managed to do a surprising amount for herself. Dan spent as much time as he could with her.

Whatever happened, she was not going to be back at school for the start of the new term. She asked Dan to write to the Head on her behalf and explain the situation. A few days later, the Head phoned Jess's mobile. She was very nice about it and said she would organise a supply teacher for the foreseeable future.

'While you're there, Stella,' Jess said,

'I should warn you that I shall be handing in my notice and leaving as soon as possible.' She explained why, including her plans for the future with Dan.

'That's so lovely, Jess. How about I advertise for temporary cover for you, with a view to a permanent position? If we're lucky enough to find someone suitable, you can leave right away. We shall be sorry to lose you, all the same.'

Dan was delighted, though her parents were disappointed she wouldn't be coming home. 'But Mum, it's all in a good cause. And it does mean we can organise the wedding for that much sooner.'

'What are you saying, Jess?'

'That's Dan's asked me to marry him and I've said yes! We're officially engaged!'

'Oh, darling, that's wonderful! How have his parents taken it?'

'He's telling them right now. We're thinking of a Christmas wedding. How does that suit?'

'Wonderful. I'll phone Kim right away and tell her. Congratulations, darling. To both of you. We couldn't be more pleased.'

'Looks like my life is now all sorted,' Jess said to Dan later that evening. 'I just need to hear from the solicitor that the charges of coercion have been dropped and that everything's cut and dried. Then we can start planning our wedding.'

'Oh, and the solicitor reckons that Poppy looking so much like me is just one of those weird coincidences. There's no way she and I could possibly be so closely related.'

'I could have told you that!' Dan grinned. 'You're sweet and lovely and she's, well, she's not. And now I have a confession to make. I'm horribly afraid that Mum's started the wedding preparations already.. I saw an order for half a ton of dried fruit being written out. I guess that's the cake organised. You don't mind, do you?'

'Better she should do it than me. You

haven't seen any of my cakes!'

There was a knock at the door. Dan answered it.

April stood outside.

'Can I come in?'

'I suppose so.'

'I brought you this.' She held out an old-fashioned exercise book. 'Me mum's diary from when she was a girl. It was hidden in her old room and I found it. But she doesn't want it now. Says she doesn't want any reminders of what she did. And me brother says he's given up trying to get anything out of May, now he's seen what Mum's diary says. Weren't May's fault. So we're moving on. We won't be troubling you again.'

She turned and left the room. Dan went to close the door after her.

Jess picked up the exercise book. It was all here. June's plans to get Derek away from her older sister, and describing in detail how she would pretend to be pregnant if all else failed.

Jess read a little of it and then

reached over and dumped it in the waste bin.

'It's all in the past now,' she said. 'But thank you, dear Auntie May. Without you and your generosity, I'd never have met Dan and had such a wonderful future to look forward to.'

'Hear, hear,' Dan agreed. 'To our future.'

'And the cat and kittens are still here, too. I can keep them now, can't I?' Jess appealed.

'OK,' Dan said with a smile, 'you've won me over. I'll love them just as much as I love you, which is an awful lot.'

And as Jess went into his arms, she could swear she could hear her little cat family purring their approval.

THE END